Flight of the Crow

Howard A Schwartz

Cover design by Margaret B Schwartz

www.HowardASchwartz.com

Acknowledgements

I would like to thank all the people who helped me with this book including my friends — Les Linster and Katy KrantzVictor; my brothers — Bill and Ron Schwartz; and especially my wife, Margaret. She is my inspiration and final editor.

ONE

SOMETIME DURING THE night, a chunk of cement forced its way inside my brain and settled behind my eyes. At least that's what it felt like. My head throbbed and I dreaded getting out of bed. I prized one eye open and glimpsed at what looked like bars of a jail cell, but it was only the morning light on the bedroom wall entering through the louvered slats of the plantation shades.

6:30 a.m.

What a night!

My blanket was rolled into a ball at the foot of my bed and my sweat-soaked pillow was lying on the floor. Seven hours used to be enough sleep for me, but ever since the incident, it hasn't felt sufficient.

Even before I moved, I knew my back and knee would be sore. I carefully peeled away my sweatshirt and pants, reached down to get my black oak cane off the floor, and finally pushed myself up off the bed.

In the process of standing up, it felt like a knife had been stuck into my spine, and a piece of coarse

4

sandpaper was dragging across my knee joint. The knee itself looked as if a one-inch notch had been chiseled out of the bone and a foot-long zipper had been tattooed down the side.

I grabbed the brace off the nightstand and secured it tightly behind my knee. As I limped toward the bathroom, a scratching noise outside the bedroom door caught my attention. Max, my four-year-old wire fox terrier stood, with his head cocked, holding his leash in his mouth. I let him in and patted the top of his head.

"Sorry, buddy." It took my breath away just to bend over. "I'll let you outside as soon as I'm done in the bathroom."

With hands braced against the sink, my reflection in the medicine cabinet mirror stared back at me. My hair was wild and scraggly, the skin around my eyes had a greenish tint, and the whites of my eyes were bloodshot red. Who was that stranger in the mirror? He looked like a monster straight out of a bad movie. *The Night of the Zombies*, starring Anthony Howard Crow!

Seven months had passed since my surgery, and my life brought to mind the old John Lennon song: *Whatever Gets You Through the Night*. Painkillers were not only a necessity, but also a way of life. I had spent four years in the United States Army, nine years as a police officer at the 5th Precinct in Minneapolis, and I'd gone through an excruciating divorce, but I'd never experienced anything as difficult as this pain and addiction.

I was both mentally and physically dependent on the pills. A normal day revolved around each opportunity to take another one, or an alcoholic drink, and sometimes both. Like all addicts, I believed I could stop at any time, never realizing how serious my addiction had become until I tried to quit several times. Finally, through some deep reserve of strength, or maybe desperation, I resolved to 'take a break' from the painkillers and tough it out like the soldier and cop I had been. For twenty-two days I stayed drug-free (although occasionally I still enjoyed a drink) and that got me over the worst part of rehab.

I'm still in a lot of pain, but slowly beginning to feel better.

***

It was seven months earlier, on a cold and snowy, late December evening, when my partner, Officer Jeff Lee, and I answered a call for a domestic dispute on Edmund Boulevard in south Minneapolis. A complaint had been phoned in about a disturbance and fighting between the caller's neighbors, Rene and Manny Garza. He told the dispatcher it sounded as if an argument had turned violent.

The neighborhood was filled with high-end houses that looked out over the Mississippi River, but the shabby condition of the house was not the norm for the neighborhood. The yards in front of the houses were on a steep incline, so I drove down the alley and parked our squad car at the back of the house, near the garage. An old cedar privacy fence enclosed the terrace and was severely rotted and about to fall over. A relentless north wind was blowing and the snow from the daylong storm was already knee high, but it still couldn't hide the rusted automobile parts and old appliances scattered across the lawn.

As we navigated our way through the banks of snow to the back of the house, Jeff shook his head with repulsion. "It's the middle of winter," he said. "Everything's frozen, but this place still smells! How's that possible?"

I removed my gloves and earmuffs, placed my ear to the door and listened. Dead silence, but my instincts knew better. I knocked loudly on the door.

"Who's there?" A man yelled from inside the house.

I inched toward the right side of the doorframe, Jeff moved to the left. "Police. Open the door!" I rested my hand on my pistol.

"Go away, everything is fine in here."

"I'm afraid we can't do that, sir."

"Did that asshole Jim Starkey call you again?"

"I couldn't tell you, even if I knew. Now please let us in."

With domestic disputes you never knew what might happen. An argument could escalate and become too loud; but if alcohol or drugs were involved, the outcome was unpredictable. I was about to knock again when I heard the sound of the door being unlocked.

A middle-aged man, looking like he needed a bath, opened the door but blocked the entryway. He wore a sleeveless grungy T-shirt, worn out blue jeans and neither shoes nor socks. On his right bicep he had a tattoo of a devil perched on a tombstone. The man's upper lip was wet with perspiration and he ran his hand through his thin black hair. From where I stood I could smell alcohol. I kept my hand on my pistol.

"Are you Manny Garza?" I asked. I moved in front of the partially open door. Jeff moved behind me.

He put his hands up. "Don't shoot me, bro," he smiled, but he appeared to be nervous.

"You need to let us in, Mr. Garza."

"Come back later, my wife is sleeping and she ain't feeling too good."

He tried to shut the door, but I managed to get my foot in the opening.

"We need to make sure everything is fine. If the call turns out to be a mistake, we'll be on our way shortly."

He opened the door, wiped his mouth with the back of his hand and stepped back.

"You're letting all the heat out, so you might as well come in." He prattled on, "That nosy neighbor of ours needs to mind his own business. We aren't bothering him at all. How can he possibly know anything that we do in our own home? We had our TV on really loud, so how could he hear anything above that?"

I looked behind the door then followed him inside. Officer Lee stayed behind me in the entryway.

The house stunk of dirt, cooking grease, and sweat. Clothes were strewn across the hardwood floors; empty beer bottles and half-eaten containers of food were everywhere. The living room was dimly lit. The only shades on the windows were blankets hanging from an improvised rope. In spite of the chill inside the house, the

8

ceiling fan was spinning, but three of the four bulbs were burnt out. There seemed to be no other lighting in the house.

"Are you Manny Garza?" I interrupted his nervous tirade.

"Yes, I am." While he spoke, he briefly glanced back over his left shoulder.

"Is there someone besides your wife in this house, sir?"

Jeff stepped in the direction where Garza had looked.

"Just my wife," he admitted and swallowed. "Man, I need to ask a favor."

"What's that, Mr. Garza?" I asked.

He moved backwards as he spoke. "Rene, that's my wife, see, well we had a fight earlier. But, everything is cool now, so could you come back later? She had too much to drink and I think she just needs to sleep it off."

Officer Lee moved to the far end of the living room and looked down the hallway. "Is your wife in one of the rooms back there?" He pointed.

Garza didn't answer.

"We'll need to see her before we can leave," I said.

"Rene! Come out here! They want to talk to you."

"Please go, I'm okay," an unseen woman yelled back. Her voice was muffled.

"That's good to hear ma'am," I called out. "But we're still going to need to speak with you in person."

Manny Garza slowly inched toward the front door and Jeff followed.

"Sir, I'm going to have to ask you to stand over

9

there." He pointed next to the buffet.

I heard the bedroom door open and Rene Garza walked out. She was wearing a red robe, her head was down, and she was shielding her face with her right hand.

"Ma'am, please look at me," I said.

She did so slowly, lifting her head. Her right eye was swollen shut and her nose was bent to the side. There was dried blood on her mouth and chin.

"Watch out! He has a gun!" She pointed at her husband and screamed.

What happened during the next 60 seconds has continued to haunt my dreams ever since.

Garza pulled out a .38 special that had been tucked inside the back of his pants. He shot two rounds into Jeff Lee's face and turned the pistol at his wife and shot her in the stomach.

Both as an officer and a soldier I had been trained to shoot at targets, but I had never shot a live round at another person.

I hesitated, and I paid for it.

Before I was able to draw my pistol from its holster, Garza fired a round into my right side, directly below my rib cage. The force of the bullet was tremendous, and I fell backwards, landing hard on the floor.

I've heard that when you're dying and about to cross over, an old friend or relative will visit and welcome you to the other side. If that's true, then I should have known I wasn't going anywhere. I lay on my back, suddenly aware of the rotating fan and the flaking   paint on the ceiling.

As it turned out, getting knocked down probably saved my life. Garza fired another bullet that narrowly missed my prostrate body. I kicked my legs up for protection and took his last round in my right knee. My memory of what took place after that is not clear. I heard later from a fellow police officer that I had returned fire six times, four of the bullets striking Manny Garza's torso. He took his last breath at the scene. Jeff Lee died on the way to the hospital, but Rene Garza survived.

I was barely able to call for an ambulance and was prepped for surgery as soon as I arrived in the emergency room at the Hennepin Medical center in downtown Minneapolis. Three specialists operated on me for a total of seven hours, and I was in the intensive care ward for an additional thirty-six hours after that. All in all, I believe I have a lot to be thankful for. Mostly, that I avoided being permanently paralyzed by a bullet that missed my spine by a quarter of an inch.

One of my biggest regrets was that I wasn't able to pay my respects to Jeff Lee at his funeral. He had been a good friend and partner for the last nine years.

***

So began my long road to recovery. The doctor responsible for my rehabilitation warned that I might not walk normally again. But after another surgery and four months of physical therapy, I could walk first with a walker, and then with a cane. For a while I couldn't drive a car because I was worried about stepping on the brake and the pain it would cause my knee. Thankfully, during rehab, my health insurance paid for transportation to the grocery store and to physical therapy.

Six months after the shooting, I still hadn't heard any news about a timetable for returning to the 5th Precinct. All the free time was making me antsy and I needed to know where I stood with the police department. I phoned my commanding officer and inquired about the possibility of returning to work. He avoided the question and instead referred me to the City of Minneapolis Human Relations department. I called the man assigned to my case and he offered me a choice: take a pension and severance package or a desk job. It was about what I had expected, but it was still difficult to hear. I couldn't see myself sitting behind a desk for the rest of my career, so I accepted the payoff.

Like many people I had often wondered what I wanted to do after retiring, but I never thought it would take place until I was at least fifty, the earliest age an officer can retire and collect benefits.

After thinking long and hard about my choices, and debating with colleagues, family and friends, I decided it was an opportunity to become a private detective. It would keep me close to the work I loved, but out of the physically taxing situations that a cop needs to be prepared for daily.

I also needed to prove to myself that I was the same man I was before the shooting.

Two

A GOOD INVESTIGATOR is like a doctor or psychologist. Each professional should know the correct questions to ask, and listen carefully to what the client is saying in order to put all the pieces together. That was one of my strengths as a police officer, and I knew it would also serve me well as an investigator. What I didn't have was knowledge about how to run my own business. So I found a short course through a business incubation service that would help me prepare during my recuperation.

Attending the seminar meant leaving the house alone for the first time since the shooting, and it turned out to be more difficult than I had imagined. Even parking in a handicap parking space wasn't helpful. I still struggled to get from the parking garage to the classroom. Every step I took resulted in sharp pain from the base of my spine down to my toes, but it was the fear of falling and not being able to get up that was mentally exhausting.

The instructor of the class spent the first two days

discussing day-to-day business practices, which was useful, but for me the third day was the most interesting, as it dealt with social networking. I already had a Facebook page to keep my friends updated on my progress after the shooting. But I hadn't realized how many other social sites were available for businesses: Pinterest, LinkedIn, Twitter, Google and many more. I planned to put them all to good use.

When the seminar was over, I celebrated by going on a short walk with Max. I'm not sure how either one of us managed to accomplish the journey. Max remembered the exact streets we used to travel, and I made it without having to stop, even though my body was rebelling.

It was a wonderful feeling to be out and among the living again.

THREE

LOCATING AN OFFICE and opening a business came together faster than expected. I ended up signing a lease for an office on Lake Street in southeast Minneapolis. It was close to the downtown area and available for a reasonable rent.

Three days later I stood at the entrance with a signed lease and a key in hand to inspect the sign that I had designed, which a local agency had painted on the window. The decorative name was written in a half circle over a drawing of a flying crow that wore a deerstalker cap: *The Crow Investigation Service.*

I must have looked like a complete idiot, puffed with pride and gawking at a sign on a vacant office door, but I couldn't have cared less. I was proud of how far I had come in seven months, and was now trying to look into the future.

Later that same morning, three telephone lines were installed and my Internet service was turned on. The only thing left for me to do was to hire a receptionist and start making some money. I was now open for business, but there were issues in my personal life that still needed to be resolved.

***

When I met my ex-wife, Amanda, she was working as a waitress at a local bar. As far as I was concerned, it was love at first sight, but she needed some convincing. We dated for six months before I asked her to marry me. She agreed, and one year later, Matthew was born. That's when my life began to fall apart.

I was raised as an only child. My father, John Crow was a well-known and decorated police sergeant in Minneapolis. When I watched him being interviewed on television, or read a story where he was quoted in the newspaper, I felt proud of his accomplishments, but as a father he was a failure. I rarely saw him when he wasn't in uniform, and when he was dressed as a civilian, I almost didn't recognize him. The responsibility to raise me fell entirely on my mother's shoulders. She did a good job considering the circumstances, but deep down I felt the reason my father was rarely at home had something to do with me.

He died at the age of 43, during a shoot-out at a convention where he was scheduled to speak. I was never told the circumstances of his death, but I remember his funeral and the number of police officers who attended, and the people who spoke about him as a hero. I also remember that neither my mother nor I cried; it felt as if we were the only people there who didn't. I was 14 years old at the time.

When Amanda and I got married, I promised myself I wouldn't be like my dad, but I quickly headed down a similar path. When I wasn't working overtime at the 5th Precinct, I worked part-time as a security guard for whoever would hire me. I could have blamed it on my DNA, but that would be a bunch of crap.

The day after Matthew turned four, Amanda asked for a divorce. She told me I wasn't fit to be a father to her child. I was devastated, but deep down I knew she was right. After the divorce, Matt and I spent every other weekend at the townhouse I had rented. We even gave our time together a name, "The big boys night out." During my recuperation I was unable to take care of him, but Amanda and Matthew did visit me while I was hospitalized. Being back to work meant it was time to get back on his schedule, after a seven-month hiatus. Matthew had celebrated his eighth birthday while I was in the hospital.

***

On Friday evening I pulled up in front of the house that Amanda and I had purchased during our first year of marriage. She received the house as a part of the divorce settlement and I moved about a mile away to a rental townhouse. When I got out of the car, all I could focus on were the seven steps leading to the front door. I had forgotten about them, but at least I could use the railing for support. I had one hand on my cane and the other one on the handrail. As I took each step, I thought about Neal Armstrong walking on the moon, one small step for Tony.... By the time I was at the door, I was out of breath.

"Tony, are you okay? You should have called from your car, I would have brought him down to you."

"I'm fine," I lied, although I appreciated her compassion.

"Come in," she responded and went back into the house.

Amanda's long black hair was damp and she wore a pink-silk blouse with a pair of tight fitting black slacks. I felt a pang of remorse as I thought she might be going on a date.

"Here are Matt's things and you have my cell phone number in case there are any problems." She turned around and called out, "Matthew, your dad is here! Hurry up, honey, I have to get going."

Matt ran down the steps, and I bent down as far as I could to give him a hug and tousle his mop of hair. "Let's get going, big guy."

I went to pick up his bag, but Amanda grabbed it first. "Matt is big enough, he can carry this." She gave him the bag, then kissed him on the cheek.

I followed him down the steps. "Where did you get that cool cane?" he turned and asked. I was sure he had seen it before, but I didn't remember him mentioning it.

"I had it custom made. Do you want to hold it?"

He took it from my hand.

"What's this?" He pointed to the letters T.H.C. that were carved in the wood.

"Those are my initials, Tony Howard Crow."

"Cool, it reminds me of the Ultima Sword!" he cried,

18

and aimed the cane toward a squirrel sitting on a branch in a tree.

"What kind of sword?" I asked.

"You know, from the Final Fantasy video game."

"Oh yeah, Final Fantasy, how could I have forgotten? Here, why don't I take that before someone gets hurt."

He handed back my cane and headed toward the car. After he climbed into the back seat, I made sure he was buckled in and limped around the car to get in the driver's side.

"Is there anything special you'd like to do this weekend?" I asked.

He shook his head.

"How does a movie and pizza sound? I'm sure Max would love the company and I know he'd appreciate a walk after a long day by himself."

His eyes brightened. "Can I hold the leash?"

Matthew, Max and I ended up having a great weekend, and we all received a little of what we wanted: Max got to go on a walk and play all day with Matthew; Matthew found a new friend, a boy who lived down the street; and I was compensated the best of all - I spent quality time with my son. I was even more thrilled when I dropped him off at his mother's house on Sunday, and he wanted to know what we were going to do the next time.

Four

THE GRAND OPENING of my office had arrived. I would have thrown a party, but there really wasn't much to celebrate, and I didn't expect many phone calls. I needed to set up my new computer and create some sort of filing and billing system. I had also placed an online ad in the help wanted section of the Sunday newspaper.

I received several phone calls, but interviewing job candidates was a new experience for me. I didn't know what questions to ask, but one of the applicants stood out. Shelley Hatcher, a 50-year-old widow. On the phone, I thought she was easy to talk with, and had a professional sounding voice. We scheduled an interview for the next morning.

Shelley arrived early and filled out an application. After she had finished, I discussed what I expected from a receptionist. "Because it will only be the two of us to start with, I really need more than just someone who answers the phone. I'd want you to learn all aspects of the business, and be able to explain it to a caller if I'm not in. You'd also be responsible for researching material for a case I might be working on, and you'll need to keep track of the billing and organizing the records."

"Almost like a Girl Friday," she offered.

I smiled. "Yes, that's a pretty good description of what I need."

I felt more comfortable with Shelley the more we talked. The other two people I had interviewed didn't feel like a good fit, and Shelley had worked as a receptionist with a firm in downtown Minneapolis. She also had a sunny smile that would make a good first impression on a client.

It might not have been the proper way to hire my first employee, but I was usually a good judge of character, so I went ahead and hired her without checking her references.

After Shelley left, I placed advertisements for my company in two neighborhood newspapers. I also began to work on my website and Facebook page. I ended a very productive day by placing a call to the 5th Precinct and talking to Sergeant O'Hara, my old boss.

It was great to speak to him again and he gave me a lot of encouragement. The good news for me was that the city of Minneapolis had recently cut its funding for the police force because of reduced tax revenues. A smaller force meant they were not able to properly investigate some of the less serious crimes. He promised that my name would be given out to anyone who requested additional assistance. In my new line of work, there was no better referral than from a police officer.

The ads I placed generated a total of fourteen calls and the majority of them were from salespeople. The lone business call I received was from Josephine Day, whose first question was to ask if I ever worked with clients on a payment schedule. She was honest and told me about the three investigation firms that had already turned her down. I needed a case to get started on and without much on my schedule, we set up an appointment for her to come in and discuss the case in person.

On Friday morning I was in the process of making coffee when my first client walked through the door. Hallelujah, I thought. I almost felt as if a horn should go off and balloons ought to fall from the ceiling.

"Josephine, nice to meet you. My name is Tony Crow. Have a seat."

Josephine Day was a heavy set African-American woman in her mid-thirties, casually dressed in gray slacks and a white blouse. She had on a gold necklace with a crucifix, and held a manila folder under her left arm.

"You the only one here?" she asked. "Where's your secretary?"

"She doesn't get in until later." In this case, later meant next week.

She sat down and set the folder on my desk. "Looks to me like you just moved in here."

Maybe I should hire her to be my new investigator.

"Tell me, what can I help you with, Josephine?"

"First off, call me Jo. Only my mother calls me Josephine."

"Okay Jo, what can I help you with?"

"Well, like I told you on the phone, I can't afford to pay right away, but I'm no deadbeat. It's just that I've run into some hard times lately."

She opened her folder and handed me a letter from the Hennepin County court. It was an official court order for someone by the name of Morley Bennett to pay Josephine Day $1287 on the first day of every month, beginning January 2009. That was more than five years ago.

"He hasn't paid me a nickel in over a year. I have to put all my money into raising my kids, and I'm falling short every month. I tell you Mister..." She stopped talking and looked around my desk.

"Crow, Tony Crow." I helped her out. "Like the bird."

"Mr. Crow," she repeated deliberately. "Morley and I never got married, but he's the father of my two kids." She paused. "I knew he was no good, but after the babies were born, what choice did I have?"

I didn't try to answer that question, just kept taking notes on my legal pad.

"The court ordered him to pay $1287 a month, based on what he made working as a contractor, but he lost that job and has quit paying child support ever since."

"Have you tried to legally enforce the agreement?" I asked.

"I did," she nodded. "I had to pay someone to serve him with papers so I could take him to court, but then he lied under oath. Morley owns a bar on the north side of Minneapolis. He keeps the ownership in his father's name and he pays himself in cash."

"It's all so neat and tidy." She brushed her hands together as if she was sweeping dirt off them. "He gets to keep his money and our kids go hungry. The judge told me it was out of his hands, and it was up to me to prove that Morley had an income that he wasn't reporting. Can you imagine that? How am I gonna prove that? Well a friend of mine told me I needed to find someone to help. I saw your ad in the Northsider newspaper and here I am. We thought you could follow him around and take pictures of him while he was at his bar."

Josephine had been watching too many detective movies. "I'm not sure that taking pictures of your ex at a bar would be of any benefit to you. We don't have to prove he owns the bar; just that he's making money and not reporting it. The Internal Revenue Service might be interested in that little tidbit."

Josephine slapped my desk with the palm of her hand. "The IRS, damn now you're talking! I like your style already!"

I picked up the folder. "May I keep this?"

"That's for you. I made a copy of everything I know about Morley, including the address of the bar he claims he doesn't own. I also included his current address, cell phone number and a copy of the original judgment from the court."

"Give me a couple of days to review this, and I'll call you when I decide the best course of action."

Josephine began to stand, then sat back down again. "You know, maybe there is something I could help you with instead of paying your fee."

"What's that?" I asked, a little concerned about what she was going to suggest.

"I don't want to hurt your feelings, but this office needs an upgrade."

She was a perceptive person.

"My brother Bernie has a decorating company in Richfield. He owes me a favor and maybe I could talk to him about doing some decorating in here." She looked around. "If you don't mind me saying, the walls in this place need some pictures, and you don't have enough furniture or any curtains on your windows. It looks as if you're running some kind of game and might need to move out quickly."

From the outset I hadn't banked on getting paid from Josephine, I just needed a case to start my career. "I'm fine with that arrangement. Just one more thing." I pulled an agreement out of my desk drawer: a document I had copied and printed from a private eye web page I had found on the Internet. "If you're going to hire me, I need you to read this and sign it."

Josephine signed the agreement without looking at it and handed it back. "Good luck and call me with any news," she said leaving my office.

After she was gone, I thought about possible options to get Morley Bennett to pay the child support. Legally there was not a lot I could do without racking up a large bill, but pressuring him behind the scenes was a different story.

It felt like a good time to call an old friend of mine

that I'd been meaning to get in touch with anyway. My first case just expedited the call.

FIVE

DON HANSON WAS a former college football player, avid weight lifter and a lead guitar player in a rock and roll band back in high school. He enjoyed any activity that involved physical contact, which included the way he played the guitar. He had also been my best friend when we were growing up.

We met in the hallway, the first day of class in ninth grade. Standing over six feet tall and weighing 220 pounds, he was kind of hard to miss, but I was even taller at six foot three. The main difference was that I weighed a meager 160 pounds. We seemed to hit it off because we were the two tallest kids at Sanford Junior High School in Minneapolis, We were close during high school, but after graduation we drifted apart. I signed up for four years in the military and Don received a full scholarship to play football at the University of Michigan.

I followed his college career and was troubled to hear that he had severely injured his right knee during his junior year, and was forced to give up the game. His goal had always been to play pro ball, so I knew he must have been devastated.

That took place about thirteen years ago and we had not stayed in touch. Two weeks prior to opening my new office, a mutual friend told me he saw Don at Kelly's bar in downtown Minneapolis. Apparently he had moved back and rented an apartment so he could take care of his ailing mother. To help make ends meet, he worked nights as a bouncer. I gave him a call and we agreed to meet for a late breakfast the following morning.

***

I arrived early at the restaurant and found a booth in the back near the kitchen. Even though I had not seen him in a long time, I recognized Don as soon as he walked through the front door. His dark hair showed a few gray strands and he had let it grow a couple of inches past his collar. He had two scars on his face, one over his eye and another on his chin. The scar over his right eye was from a puck during a hockey game at Longfellow Park, and the larger scar on his chin he had obtained during a fight after a high school football game.

Don's football weight had fluctuated between 230-245 pounds, but now he looked to be at least 300, and not much of that was fat. A few people turned their heads and stared as he walked past their table.

"Big Fella!" he called out and waved when he saw me. He walked over to where I was sitting and slid into the booth seat across from me. "I was glad to hear from you. I would have called but I wasn't sure you'd want to speak to me."

"Why not?" I asked.

"When I returned to the states, I never looked you up." He paused. "And I guess I left town kind of abruptly."

"That was a long time ago, let's talk about something more recent, like what have you been up to lately?"

"Where do I begin?" he laughed.

He began with the depression he had suffered when he realized he'd never be able to play professional football.

"I moved to the Big Island of Hawaii to get away."

"That's not a bad place to get away to."

"I liked living there, but I was never able to find a decent job, and I was getting bored lying on the beach all day."

He paused for a drink of water. "I decided to see more of the world and live somewhere that was different from Hawaii; so I joined the Peace Corps."

"The Peace Corps?"

"Yeah, I know. I thought it was going to be like the movies we used to watch when we were kids. After I finished the interview process, they offered me a job in Mozambique. You know the famous saying, be careful what you wish for? That was the way I felt when I first arrived, but then I got to know some of the English-speaking locals. I decided that as long as I was there, I should put my heart into it, and as it turned out, Mozambique was a great place for me to quit feeling sorry for myself."

"Mozambique," I repeated. "What was it like?"

"Different. Living in the United States you can get anything you want by driving to the mall or a grocery store, but over there, families have to send someone out every morning with a bucket just to get water. Or if anyone gets sick, they have to walk for miles and wait in a long line to see a doctor. I watched people die, and I learned a lot, but I wouldn't do it again."

"What kinds of things did you learn?"

"Whoever has the most money and the greatest number of weapons wins." He moved uncomfortably in his seat. "I heard stories about good men and women killed in countries all over the continent, but few people in the United States ever heard anything about it because - besides Nigeria - Africa doesn't produce oil. The atrocities some of those governments got away with made me sick. Another thing I learned was that you do whatever you have to do, to survive."

It was obvious that my friend had changed a great deal since the last time I saw him. But then, so had I.

A waiter came to our table and we both ordered.

"What's this I heard about you being a cop? I never thought it would happen, but you turned out to be a chip off the old block."

I showed him my cane. "Ex-cop is more like it, but that's what I want to talk to you about."

I condensed the last thirteen years of my life into about thirty minutes, starting with the military and ending with my new business.

"You need any help?" he asked.

I nodded. "I do, but there's a catch."

"I'm listening."

"You'll only be able to work part-time for a while. The business is new and not making any money, but I can pay you a wage based on the number of hours you work."

"How much are we talking about?"

"For now, how does $20 per hour sound? It's not much, but we can negotiate that later as things pick up."

"It's more than I'm making as a bouncer." He paused and drummed his fingers on the table. "Will I be able to keep my bouncer job working nights?"

"I don't have a problem with that for now, but as we get busier, that might change. "

"Then, when do I start?"

"I was hoping you'd say that."

I told Don about my client, Jo Day, and what might occur when we confronted Morley Bennett at his bar.

"Today my plan is to drive over to the bar to get a feel for the surroundings. I'll call you tonight and let you know what I decide, but keep tomorrow open on your calendar."

Six

AFTER I HAD finished eating with Don, I drove to Morley's bar, sat in my car and watched the entrance. The name of the establishment was Teasers Grill; a strip club that served food. I watched for about thirty minutes and noticed that their daytime business was slow, so I got out of my car and headed inside. There was one man at the door checking identification, and as far as I could tell, there was only one bartender.

The interior of the bar was dimly lit. Even though it was the middle of the day and the sun was shining, you'd never know it inside. Small incandescent lights were inlaid into a plywood ceiling, softly lighting the service bar. A single spotlight beamed down on an oval dance floor. There weren't any dancers at the time, but a scantily-clad woman sat on a stool sipping a cocktail. She was either on break or waiting for enough paying customers to arrive.

I sat down at the bar and ordered a tap beer. When the bartender brought it to me, I started a conversation.

"Is this usually how busy it is here during the day?"

He looked around the bar and nodded. "During the week, we don't get crowded until after 9:00 p.m."

I continued with small talk, then paid for the beer and left a tip. On my way out I asked a question of the man who was checking identifications at the door. "What time does Morley Bennett usually get in?"

"It varies, but more times than not, he's here by 1:00 p.m. and stays until we close."

"Thanks," I replied and walked to my car.

That evening, I called Don to discuss my plan. "I'm going to confront him about the money he owes my client and there's no telling how he'll react."

"What do you want me to do?"

"That's going to depend on Morley Bennett. I need you to observe, step in if he gets violent, otherwise just use your better judgment."

We decided to meet in front of the bar the next day, and Don sounded excited.

I was parked across from the bar, sipping a coffee, when Don pulled up behind me in a blue Volkswagen bus. He got out of his van and sat in the passenger seat of my car. He showed up wearing a black Motley Crew T-shirt and dark sunglasses with silver frames shaped like snakes.

"Where did you get the VW?"

"Bought it at a used car lot. I always wanted one."

His game face was on and he stared straight ahead through my windshield as he spoke.

"Tell me again what you want me to do."

"Mostly observe. I'm not sure how Bennett will react when I confront him, but if it turns ugly I might need your help."

He nodded. "Are there limits on how much force to use?"

"Hopefully you won't have to use any. Who knows? Maybe when I explain the reason I'm here, he'll write a check for the amount he owes Jo Day and I'll be on my way."

"You don't expect that to happen, do you?"

I shook my head. "Let's play it by ear, but I'm sure it won't be that easy. The other possibility is that he throws me out of the bar. If that happens, I want you to watch him to see if he does anything that we can use to our advantage. Use your better judgment, but don't overreact. I know that's all a bit vague, but these things are complex."

"I'm getting your drift."

"Stay here, then in about 10 minutes go inside and have a seat at the far side of the bar and order a drink."

I got out of the car and walked into Teaser's Grill.

The same bartender I had yesterday was working, so I sat at his station.

"Looks like we have a regular," he said. "What can I get you today?"

"Tap beer, same as yesterday."

He brought my drink and set it on a napkin in front of me. "How about something to eat? The hamburgers here are pretty good."

I have rules I live my life by, and one of them is I

34

never eat food where naked people have been dancing. "Not right now." I leaned my cane against the bar and tried to make myself comfortable. "Morley Bennett working today?"

"You know Morley?"

I shrugged my shoulders. "Let's just say he's a friend of a friend."

He glanced around the bar. "As a matter of fact that's him over there. You want me to tell Morley you're looking for him?"

"Whenever you get the chance," I said and took a sip of my beer.

The bartender ducked under the bar ledge, and walked to where Morley was standing. I saw him point in my direction then he walked back to the bar.

I nursed my drink and gazed up at a mirror that hung over the length of the bar. That might come in handy later, as I could see who was behind me. After a short time, I saw Don enter and walk to the far side of the bar. Then Morley approached me. "I hear we have a mutual friend."

Morley Bennett was a light-skinned black man with a shaved head and a circle mustache and beard. I wasn't an expert on diamonds, but the stone in his right earlobe was probably worth as much as the child-support payments he owed my client.

"I believe we do," I answered.

"Ricky told me you wanted to speak with me, right?"

I took a drink of my beer and nodded. "I have important business I'd like to discuss."

"No time like the present."

I set my glass on the bar and wiped my lips with a napkin. "I'm here to collect the money you owe my client."

"Is that so?" He raised an eyebrow. "And who might that be?"

"Josephine Day."

"Are you shittin' me?" He pounded his fist on the bar. "Fuck that bitch." He laughed and turned away, then stopped and walked back.

"Are you her new boyfriend or something?" he asked. "I didn't know Jo liked white boys."

I pulled my business card from my shirt pocket and handed it to him.

He barely glanced at it before tossing it across the bar. "Tony Crow, Private Investigations. Is that supposed to impress me?" He paused and grabbed the edge of the bar with both hands. "Ricky says you walk with a limp. What happened to your leg Mr. P.I.?"

"I didn't come here to talk about myself. What I want to work out with you is how you're going to pay the money you owe Josephine."

Morley Bennett bent over until his face was next to mine. He was so close I could smell garlic and tobacco on his breath. "Look asshole, do you really think you can walk in my bar and try to intimidate me? How would you like a broken kneecap on your good leg?" He laughed demonstratively as if he had an audience. "Who knows? With two bad legs you might not even have a limp."

36

He looked around the bar and raised his hand. "Mike," he snapped his fingers. "Usher this asshole out of here."

In the mirror I could see a baldheaded man with a tattoo of a lightening bolt over his right eyebrow. He wore sunglasses even though the bar was dark and his navy blue sports jacket appeared to be about two sizes too small. He sauntered to the bar and stopped directly behind my stool. "Right this way, sir." He grabbed my arm.

As I was being escorted out, Bennett called from behind me. "If I ever see you in here again, next time I won't be so nice."

I allowed Mike to lead me to the door, and glanced back into the dim room. Don was standing at the far end of the bar. In front of him was a cocktail glass with a slice of pineapple and a tiny red umbrella sticking out the top.

He was speaking to a waitress but must have sensed that I was watching. He turned in my direction and nodded as I left.

SEVEN

AS SOON AS I got up the next morning, I called Don and left a message on his phone to find out what happened with Morley. I didn't hear back from him, so he was either still sleeping or had gone into work. I sent a text message and received a return text with hardly any explanation.

Mission accomplished, I think. I'll call you later and explain.

I never heard from him during the day, but I received a call from my client, as I was about to leave.

"What'd you do?" Josephine Day squealed in my ear. She was excited, but I couldn't tell if it was because she was furious or pleased.

"What happened?" I asked. I couldn't admit it, but I was curious myself.

"I just received a hand delivered letter from Morley. He apologized for being behind with his payments, and there was even a check for $1287 in the envelope. Mr. Crow, you're a doll! How did you get him to pay so fast?

I didn't think I was gonna hear from you for at least a couple of weeks."

I was upset that Don hadn't told me. I made a point to speak to him and explain how critical it was to keep me informed in a timely manner. I didn't like talking to a client and sounding like a fool. "How I did it isn't important, but I'm pleased you finally got some of the money he owes you."

"Don't worry, I plan to come through with my half of the bargain. Will you be around tomorrow? I've already spoken with my brother."

I didn't have to look at my schedule to know I was free. "I'll be here. Bernie can stop by anytime."

After I hung up, I pondered what might have taken place after I left the bar. As a police officer I had often arrested people who I knew were guilty, but they were still able to escape prosecution. The first couple of times it happened, I was frustrated, but I soon learned that police officers could only arrest a suspect and gather evidence – after that it was in the hands of a district attorney, judge and jury.

The rules I was now playing by were different. There was no such thing as "beyond a reasonable doubt." A police officer was legally restricted by the law and needed a search warrant to enter a suspect's home to look for stolen goods. For a private investigator, that wasn't necessary and we could even make a citizen's arrest. Did that mean I had more leeway to get a job accomplished? I had to give it more thought, but one thing for sure was that my client was delighted with the outcome. Should it concern me how it was accomplished?

Whatever Don did seemed to have worked, but I was still uncomfortable not knowing what his methods were.

When I was at home that night I finally heard from Don. "Sorry I didn't call you, but I pulled a double shift at the bar."

"Let's talk about that later. Tell me what happened."

"After they threw you out, I sat at the bar and studied Bennett. It was obvious that you'd aggravated him. He began to pace back and forth and then he pulled some kind of dried plant from underneath the bar and lit it on fire. It was weird. I thought the smoke might turn the sprinklers on. He waved it in the air as he walked around the section where you were seated. It reminded me of incense during a church service, except it smelled just like marijuana. I asked the bartender and he told me Bennett was burning sage. Apparently it's a Native American tradition that helps get rid of evil spirits. I watched the Shona people in Mozambique do something similar with a local herb they grew. They believed that their deceased ancestors returned as good or bad spirits. I'm not aware of Native American beliefs, but the bartender told me that Bennett believes in evil spirits, and he thinks they visit him at the bar. That got me thinking."

"It was still early, so I drove to a drugstore and bought a couple of tubes of paint. I went home and drew three stripes across my nose and underneath my eyes. When it started to get dark, I drove back to the bar and

40

waited in the parking lot. When I saw Bennett lock up, I followed him down the street to where he parked his car. He uses a private garage."

"Why did you paint stripes on your face?"

"If Bennett believed in evil spirits, then I wanted him to think I was the devil."

"A 300 pound evil spirit," I swallowed. "Go on."

"Anyway, I waited for him to open the garage door and before he got into his car, I walked up from behind, wrapped my forearm around his throat and cut off the blood flow to his brain. He struggled a bit, but I kept the pressure on until his body went limp. I made sure he was still breathing, then I wrapped his arms and legs together with duct tape and put a strip over his mouth. After that, I waited until he was conscious."

"What happened then?"

"As soon as I heard him moan, I pulled him closer so he could see my face, then I explained why he was in that position. I reminded him that he was the father of two great kids who were depending on him, and I told him how my dad had abandoned me when I was a child. I looked directly into his eyes and asked, 'Do you really want your kids to grow up to be like me?"

"Your dad didn't abandon you. Leroy was a great father."

"I know that, but Bennett didn't. Anyway I'm pretty sure he understood what I was saying."

"If his mouth was taped shut, how could you have known that?"

"He pissed in his pants."

41

"Yeah," I cleared my throat. "It sounds like he received the message."

"Before I left, I warned him that if I found it necessary to return because he didn't do the right thing, I'd stick him under one of the tires on his car, shift it to neutral and give it a push down the driveway." Don paused to bring himself back into the present. "How did it work out?"

"You got your point across, Josephine received a check today."

"Great, that was even faster than I thought. I would like to have seen the look on the face of the person who found him the next morning. Anyway, I know you didn't get paid from your client, so my first assignment was on the house, but from now on the meter is running at $20 per hour. Let me know when we can get together and discuss any future work you might have."

"That's a good idea."

I had to admit Don was able to get the result I had hoped for, but his unorthodox methods made me uneasy. It was something I had to think about before my next job.

***

The next morning, Bernie Day from Bernie's Home Decorating showed up at my office. We walked through the reception area as he took note of the blank walls and described what he wanted to do. Before leaving, he measured the total square footage of each room and promised he'd return the next day.

Besides that, it was an uneventful day. I returned a few phone calls and updated my web pages. It had taken me three weeks from the time I opened my office until I solved my first case, and for that I was happy. From the number of calls I was receiving, there would soon be more on the horizon.

Hopefully some of them would even be able to pay.

Eight

BERNIE, ALONG WITH one of his assistants, was waiting when I arrived the next morning. It took them about three hours to carry the new furnishings into my office and rearrange it. When he had finished, I was impressed. The improvements included a roll top desk in a corner of the reception area, a brown circular rug in front of the couch, and two small wooden end tables with an art deco lamp on each of them. The formerly bare walls now sported still life paintings in each office, and a drawing of Sherlock Holmes smoking his signature meerschaum pipe next to the entryway. Everything was coming together. I had my first happy client and a professional looking office.

On Monday, my new receptionist, Shelley Hatcher, arrived for her first day of work. I liked the way she immediately took charge and arranged her workplace to enhance the flow: feng shui is what she called it, and a bagua map was a tool she used to understand the areas in the office that apparently lacked good chi. I'm not implying Shelley didn't know what she was talking about, but I sure-as-hell didn't. I stood in the corner of the room, nodding my head as if I understood and tried not to get in her way.

She also appeared to be a fast learner, and only heard me speak about my service a couple of times before she was able to describe it almost as well as I did. That would be a big help, allowing me to spend more time out of the office working on cases.

Calls from prospective clients continued to increase to the point where I even turned down a few jobs. Most of them were from people who suspected their spouses of cheating. There was money to be made in those types of cases, but I didn't like the idea of running around with a camera spying on people; it felt too voyeuristic. Unless I needed the money, I'd concentrate on cases I was more comfortable with.

NINE

SHELLEY HAD SCHEDULED an early appointment on Thursday at 7:00 a.m. That was the only time Greta Bergren could come to my office. She wouldn't tell Shelley what she wanted to talk about, insisting that she'd only speak with me in person. I arrived early and started the coffee machine.

She walked in promptly at 7:00 a.m., a good-looking but imposing, six-foot tall redhead, dressed all in gray. There was nothing frivolous about Greta, and I turned on my best manners. "Ms. Bergren, have a seat. Would you like a cup of coffee or a glass of water?"

"Coffee, black, thank you."

I made small talk about the weather as I poured fresh coffee into two cups. Since I had to use my cane with one hand I could only bring one cup at a time. Greta made no move to help and seemed content to look around the office with a poker-faced expression.

Finally I eased into my chair and looked at Greta across my desk. "So, what can I help you with this morning?"

She took a business card from the holder on my desk. "I'm representing someone who'd like to remain anonymous for the time being."

"Shelley told me that, but before I agree to take anyone as a new client, I have to know who I represent and what they're asking me to do."

"I understand."

"By the way, how did you get my name?"

"Sergeant O'Hara at the 5th Precinct. You come very well recommended."

I made a mental note to give my old sergeant a call and thank him for the referral.

"Mr. Crow, my boss is a public person." She cleared her throat and sat straight in the chair. "When you hear his name, you'll recognize it immediately. He'd like to speak to you about locating a missing person, but it's important that you keep the information from the public."

"I understand. For whom should I start searching?" I picked up a pad of paper and pen.

Over the next fifteen minutes, I heard a story about a well-to-do married man who cheated on his wife, broke up with his mistress and later regretted it. The only item Greta left out was the gentleman's name and the name of the woman I'd be searching for.

"That's why we need your help. We want you to locate this woman."

"Has she left the state?"

She shook her head. "We have no way of knowing,

but she has friends who live in the south."

"And I'd be given that information?"

"Everything we know, but only after we reach an agreement for your services."

"What other information do you have that might help me locate her?"

"Her social security number, driver's license number and her last known address in Minnesota."

"I'm honored that you called me, but why not hire one of the larger investigation firms to locate her? This would be a breeze for one of them."

"We'd prefer a discreet investigation. A large firm would also mean more employees, and as hard as they might try, the information could possibly leak." She folded her hands on her lap. "We've done our due diligence on your past record. You were a quality public servant and come highly recommended. We have faith that you can find her, but I wouldn't be telling the truth if I told you that was the only reason you were chosen. Your company is just starting out and that means it will not be burdened with a large caseload. If you decide to work with us, we'll demand your undivided attention. Also, with fewer employees, the chances of a leak will be that much less."

That sounded reasonable, but I was sure there was more to it. A large and well-established company would be more difficult to discredit if information was leaked that turned out to be damaging. With me, it would be my word against theirs.

"A year is a long time," I stated. "She might be

married by now."

Greta nodded. "We understand, and if that's the way it turns out, he'll have to deal with it."

"What's the next step?"

"My boss would like to meet you in person. If that goes well, you can discuss your fee. If not, he'll pay you for the time you spent at the meeting and you can both go your separate ways."

"I'm interested."

"Great, then we'll be in touch." Greta Bergren stood up to walk out, but paused. "One more thing. Before you can meet, you'll be required to sign a non-disclosure agreement."

"I don't have a problem with that."

"Good. I'll email you the agreement as soon as I get back to my office. Have a nice day." She picked up her purse and headed toward the door.

TEN

I HAD TWO messages from my answering service when I came in to work on Friday morning. One was from Don; he wanted to know when we could get together. The other message was from Greta Bergren. I called her first.

"I spoke to my boss and he'd like to meet you at 1:00 p.m."

"Today?"

"If that's convenient."

"I'll make it work, give me his address."

"That won't be necessary. A car will be waiting outside your office at 1:00 p.m., but first we need you to sign the non-disclosure agreement I spoke to you about yesterday. I've already emailed it to you. Read it, and if everything meets your approval, sign it and fax it back."

"What if I have a question?"

"It's a standard agreement that's signed by all his employees, and it is non-negotiable. If there is anything that you can't live with, we'll have to find someone else."

I checked my email and the contract was waiting for me. I printed it off, returned to my desk and read through it. Most of it was legal mumbo jumbo but the general idea was that the agreement protected the confidentiality of information that was to be disclosed during the meeting or possible employment. The penalty for the disclosure would be ascertained by a court of law, which could mean just about anything. I was concerned about that item, but what took me by surprise was one of the two names at the bottom of the agreement: Anthony H. Crow and Raymond R. Gilbert. I hesitated for a second because I was shocked to see the other name, and knew that I was dealing with a very powerful man. I quickly signed it and faxed it back.

I returned Don's call and tried not to speculate about the man I was going to meet.

"Big Fella," he croaked when he answered.

"Did I wake you?"

"Don't worry about it, I had to get up to answer the phone."

Oldest joke in the book, but it still made me grin. "When do you want to get together and discuss your job description?"

"What time is it now?"

"8:00 a.m."

"Let me take a shower, get something to eat and I'll be at your office by 11:00."

This time when Don walked in the door I almost didn't recognize him. He was a man of many disguises. Today he wore a brown sports jacket, tan pants and a

51

yellow flannel shirt. It also appeared as if he had cut his hair, but when he sat down I saw that he had tied it in a ponytail and tucked it underneath his collar.

"I'm impressed, I think."

"I figured if we're going to be discussing my new job, I should do my best to look professional. I don't own a sports jacket so I stopped at a Goodwill store on my way here. These are the only clothes they had that were in my size."

"What is your size?"

"52 long."

"Well, that means there's at least one other guy your size in Minnesota."

"Anyone ever tell you, that you should've been a comedian?"

I began by discussing what I expected of Don as an investigator and the importance of keeping me informed of his activities. "My police experience met the requirements in the state of Minnesota to get a P.I. license, so you can work under me as an intern, but I think it would be a good idea for you to get your own license someday. Before you can take the test, you'll have to work 6,000 hours to qualify. Until then, it's my neck on the line and I'll be responsible for you."

Don scratched his cheek. "I understand and I'm cool with it. I think we'll make great partners someday."

"As long as you understand that we're not partners now."

"I do."

"Finally I don't want our friendship to get in the way

of doing high quality work. My job and this company is what's important to me right now."

"Being friends won't be a problem. If it is, I'll step away."

"Sounds good." I stood up and grabbed my cane. "Follow me."

I headed down a short hallway to the smaller of the two offices. "You can use this space."

Don smiled and walked around the room with his fingertips touching the walls. "My own office." He stopped and cracked his knuckles. "Can I hang some of my pictures on the walls? I did some painting during my free time in Mozambique."

Painting? My friend continued to amaze me. I had never thought of Don as a painter. "It's your office, you can do what you'd like. Just remember that you might have to meet with our clients in here."

At 12:55 p.m. my cell phone rang. A woman informed me that there was a car waiting in front of my office. I hung up and told Don what I needed to do. I grabbed my briefcase and he followed me as I walked outside.

A chauffeur got out of a black Lincoln Town Car.

"Mr. Crow?" He looked at Don.

Don smiled and pointed to me. As he walked toward his car, he gave me a salute.

"I'm Tony Crow," I said to the driver.

"My name is Henry. I'm here to drive you to a meeting."

He opened the back door and waited for me to get in.

We drove west on Lake Street, then north on Hennepin Avenue, past Lake of the Isles, took the Highway 394 ramp and headed west until it changed to State Highway 12. From there he turned off on Highway 15 and headed to Wayzata. My mind drifted off as I deliberated about the man I was about to meet.

The Gilbert family was a legend in Minnesota. When I was a kid, and had saved enough money from my paper route, I'd sneak away and take a city bus to shop at Gilbert's in downtown Minneapolis. I was eleven years old and it was the summer before I started sixth grade. I had to go without permission from my parents, because I knew they'd never allow me to take a bus downtown on my own.

My family didn't have a lot of money, so I had to pretend to be interested in buying a sweater or jacket. That was the only way that they'd let me try them on. It was my way to fantasize about an alternate lifestyle. If a salesperson asked me where my parents were, I'd point to a couple on the other side of the store. Gilbert's clothing was considered to be high-end boutique and was not a luxury my parents could afford.

***

Henry turned down an asphalt driveway and paused to wait for a security gate to open. As we continued toward Lake Minnetonka, the asphalt road changed to brick and an eight-foot privacy hedge emerged on both sides of the driveway. The car stopped next to an attached five-car garage, where a man was washing a Ford Model T in one of the stalls.

54

The Gilbert residence on the southern tip of Bracketts point of Lake Minnetonka was one of the more prestigious pieces of land in Minnesota. The Gilbert family had built and owned the 28,000 square foot house since the early 1900s. It was part of Minnesota folklore that many were familiar with.

The sizable brick mansion looked more like an old hotel than a single-family house. The roof was covered with red ceramic tile and was peaked with two circular towers. A gray stone fountain with cascading water was positioned near the back door entryway. A statue of an angel sat at the top of the waterfall, playing a harp while it looked up toward the sky.

Henry got out and opened my door.

"Mr. Gilbert is at the pool and he's expecting you." He pointed toward the back of the house. "I'll wait here and drive you back as soon as you're finished."

I followed the sound of a man's voice until I came to an Olympic-sized swimming pool. The voice belonged to Ray Gilbert, the current lieutenant governor of Minnesota and largest stockholder for the Gilbert's store chain. With over 200 stores in the U.S. alone, his personal fortune was estimated to be over three billion dollars.

I recognized him from the stores' advertising during the holidays, and more recently on television during the political debates. He seemed larger in person. He wore navy blue pants with a light blue shirt and red tie. His hair was mostly gray and even though I knew he was in his early 50's, he appeared to be younger. He was talking on his cell phone when I arrived.

He acknowledged me as soon as I entered the pool area. "Mr. Crow. I'll be with you shortly." He then promptly walked away.

I stared in his direction as he paced around the pool.

"Hello?" I heard him say. He removed the phone from his ear and looked at the screen. It appeared as if he had lost his connection. "Damn it," he mumbled and walked into his house.

A minute or two later he reappeared. He was biting his lower lip and looked peeved as he walked toward me. "I'm Ray Gilbert," he reached over and we shook hands. "I want to apologize in advance, but I've got a really strange request. My cell phone just went dead as I was finishing up a very important call. I went into my house to see if I could use my wife's phone, but she's speaking overseas to a friend."

I nodded. "I can wait."

"Well, thank you for that," he smiled. "But what I want to ask is if I could use your cell phone, for a couple of minutes. I assure you that the call is local and I'll be more than happy to pay for any charges. I know this is an unusual request, but I'm in a bit of a bind."

Loaning my cell phone to a stranger was not something I'd made a habit of doing, but I was talking to the lieutenant governor and I also wanted to make a good first impression. I pulled the phone out of my pocket, typed in the password and passed it to him.

"Thank you, it will be just a moment."

I watched him push in a phone number then begin to talk. He walked back into his house, and I lost the sound of his voice for a few minutes. Within about five minutes he returned and gave me the phone back.

"I'm sorry about that, but there was an emergency at my office and I couldn't have waited until my phone was recharged. Have a seat." He pointed to a black cast-iron table and chairs next to the pool. "I'll be right back."

I thought about asking him why he didn't use his phone while it was being charged, but maybe he was the type of guy who had to walk while he was thinking.

I sat and gazed at the remarkable 180-degree view of the greenish-blue water of Lake Minnetonka. The sun reflected through the 100-year-old oak and maple trees that surrounded his house. Two fishing boats drifted within twenty feet of shore, and a double decker yacht floated near a small island. The scene would have made an excellent oil painting and I had to remind myself that we were only 20 minutes from downtown Minneapolis.

Gilbert stepped outside. "My wife would rather we meet inside, if that is okay with you."

I used the arms of my lounge chair to push myself up, trying not to grunt from the effort. "That's fine." I followed him through the porch and into a large living room.

"Make yourself comfortable, I'll go get her."

While I waited for Gilbert and his wife, I admired some of the antiques that were displayed on shelves and structures throughout the room. Most of them were artifacts from American history, including the Civil War, but the collection that attracted my interest could be seen through the glass doors of a mahogany cabinet. The cabinet itself was old and probably considered to be a valuable antique, but it was the contents that drew my attention. Inside was a collection of German World War II memorabilia. As in a museum, there was a brief description under each item. The middle shelves were filled with Nazi officers' belt buckles and helmets, and the lower shelf held a single BDM dagger, otherwise known as the blade of the Hitler youth.

In a history class at high school, I remember reading about the Nazi youth camps that trained and indoctrinated the German children, but to see a weapon that was designed for one of Hitler's future "Aryan Supermen" sent a shiver up my spine.

The only item in the cabinet without a description was a gold ring that was resting on a red-velvet cloth. I was squinting to read the insignia, when Gilbert re-appeared, with his wife walking behind him.

"Are you interested in World War II collectibles Mr. Crow?" he asked.

"A little, but I've never seen a collection like you have here."

"I just acquired that one." He took a set of keys from his pocket, opened the cabinet, removed the ring off of the fabric and handed it to me. "There are 16 rubies in the center of the ring that form a swastika, and seventeen oak leaves flank two swords on each side. It was owned by Adolf Hitler."

I almost dropped the ring when I heard that name. I set it back on the display, and wiped my hands on my pants.

"Well, he can't hurt you now," Gilbert joked. "All the other items in the cabinet were brought back by our brave boys after the war ended. I also love United States history, and I've filled an entire warehouse with Americana collectibles - if you're interested I can show them to you sometime."

Before I had a chance to answer, Gilbert's wife cleared her throat.

"I'm sorry, Mr. Crow, this is my wife, Gloria."

"Please, call me Tony." I stepped forward to shake her hand, but she ignored it.

"If you two men would rather talk shop, I have more important things to do." She made a move to walk away, but Gilbert reached out and took her arm.

Gloria Gilbert appeared to be a couple of years younger than her husband. Her skin was tan, she had short gray hair and looked as if she kept herself in good shape. As far as I knew, she was not a public person and did her best to stay out of the limelight.

"I thought it was important that you meet us both in person. I want you to understand that I keep no secrets from Gloria."

"How can I help?" I asked.

Ray Gilbert gestured. "Please, have a seat."

I sat down on a brown leather chair and they sat on a matching sofa across from me. Gilbert placed his hands on his knees, bent his shoulders forward and exhaled deeply. When he started his story he was staring at me with intense brown eyes.

He related that the first 25 years of their life together

were happy ones. Gloria was from a well-to-do family that owned a national chain of lumberyards, and the Gilbert household was one of the most affluent families in Minnesota. "We married after dating for 13 months," he asserted, "and have had four wonderful kids and three grandchildren. But like most married couples, we've had our share of difficult times that we've had to work through." He paused and brushed his fingers across his mouth. "I admit that I made an error in judgment when I had an affair with one of my employees, Marsha Cummings."

The story he told was a familiar one: a deceiving husband who cheated with a younger woman because she made him feel young again. When his wife discovered what was going on, she threatened to divorce him. He immediately stopped seeing his mistress, who took the breakup hard. She quit her job with his company and moved away.

"I haven't seen her nor heard from her in over a year, and I'm extremely concerned about her well-being."

"Why?" I asked. "You were the one who broke off the relationship."

Gilbert glanced at his wife, then back at me. "I still care for her. If you locate her and she doesn't want anything to do with me, then I'll be forced to accept it. But I want a chance to explain myself."

Well, that was not the answer I had expected. I glanced at Gloria to see what her reaction was. She was stoic, sitting with her hands in her lap and showed no emotion.

"Have you made an attempt to contact any of Marsha's family members or friends?"

He nodded. "Her parents have both passed away and Marsha is an only child. I've called the two friends of hers that I'm aware of, but neither have heard from her since she quit." He paused to gather his thoughts. "But I'm not sure that I believe them. In the mental state Marsha was in when she left, I'm certain she gave them instructions not to speak to me."

"What makes you think I could find her?"

"I'm not sure you can, I'm not sure anyone can, but I have to start somewhere."

"Does that mean I'm the only private detective you've contacted?"

"I've been agonizing over this decision for the last couple of months." He looked at his wife. "After discussing it with Gloria, we both feel that this is the correct way to handle the situation."

I turned my attention toward his wife. "Mrs. Gilbert, what do you think of your husband searching for an ex-lover? This has to be strange for you."

If her eyes could shoot bullets, my face would have been bleeding.

"I've come to terms with our marriage. Ray will be able to avoid a very messy and expensive divorce…and I get to keep what I love about this lifestyle. He's the lieutenant governor now, but there is more in his future. I see the way the public adores him, and even though our marriage is a sham, we both agree that I should be part of it."

61

"I find that surprising," I remarked.

She made no effort to compose herself. "So much of any political life is pretentious and theatrical. For whatever reason, voters in this country do not respect a politician who's been divorced. You see it in the news on a regular basis: a prominent legislator is caught cheating with an employee or a prostitute. He denies it at first, but when the evidence mounts up, he tries to turn it around so that it appears as if he was the victim. Then he holds a press conference and lo and behold, who is that woman standing next to him? His wife. Do you really believe that a woman, who's been shamed and embarrassed, would want to be standing next to the man who had cheated on her? Please..." She exhaled loudly and brushed her hair with her fingers. "Spare me your righteous indignation, Mr. Crow; this is just another act in the great American play called U.S. Politics."

I was tempted to ask how she really felt, but had the feeling neither of them were in the mood for joking.

It was obvious that Gilbert didn't appreciate what his wife had disclosed. His face was red, but he quickly recovered. "Before we go any further, are there any questions that you have for me?"

"Yes, two...the first one is, why did you call me? I was told it was a referral from Sergeant O'Hara at the 5th Precinct, but how did the two of you meet?"

"I've always made a habit of being friends with our law enforcement men and women." He clasped his hands together and smiled. "But I also knew your father John Crow. I wouldn't say we were friends, but more like acquaintances. I met him at a couple of fundraisers and I followed his career. He was a great man and someone you should be proud of."

"Thank you, I am." I wasn't surprised by his reaction. I had spoken to a lot of people over the years who seemed to know more about my father than I did.

"The second question is more of a personal one. I'm familiar with the Gilbert family and the success of your stores. I also know that you're a wealthy man. If you don't mind me asking, why did you go into politics?"

"There are times that I've wondered that myself," he responded. "I'll be the first to admit that I was born with a silver spoon in my mouth. I've been very, very fortunate, and I guess it's my way to give back to the people who've not been as blessed as I have. That's sounds like a cliché but it's true, and there is no other way for me to describe it. I know I could just sit back and read or fish all day, but I'm not ready for that. I want to do some good and try to help the people who cannot help themselves."

I nodded because I didn't know what else to say. It was obvious that I was speaking to a skilled politician. All that was missing was God Bless America playing softly in the background.

I told Gilbert that I'd be interested in taking the case and informed him of my fee - $125 per hour plus expenses. I would also require a $10,000 retainer to get started. He didn't bat an eye.

"Call my receptionist." He handed me his card. "A check will be waiting for you at my office, and you'll have a copy of all the information that I've been able to gather on Marsha."

We stood up and shook hands, but Gloria Gilbert had already left the room.

Henry drove me back to my office. I was ecstatic about having my first major case, but I couldn't help but feel as if a teacher or parent had just lectured me. Ray Gilbert sounded like every other politician who makes the rounds on the Sunday morning talk shows. They all use the same hand gestures when they speak, and they always want to help the little guy. It makes me wonder why, with so much help promised by both of the political parties, the less fortunate continue to grow in number.

ELEVEN

I KNEW FROM my nine years as a police officer, and the brief time I've spent as a private detective, that being right or wrong wasn't always as black and white as it appeared to be on television or in the movies. A case I worked on this week helped to prove my point.

I received a call from Harvey Goldthorpe, the owner of the Bryant Avenue Grocery store near Lake Calhoun in south Minneapolis. He told me about some money that was disappearing from his safe at work. "Every morning when I open the store," he said, "the first thing I do is to check the previous day's receipts against the cash that was left in the safe. I've never had a problem until a couple of months ago. At first the difference was small, $20, so I thought that someone had made a mistake and didn't give it any more thought, but it was short $25 a week later. I questioned the employee who closed up the night before, but she denied knowing anything about it. I've come to the conclusion that someone in the neighborhood is waiting for us to close, then breaking in and taking money from the safe."

Harvey's theory didn't make sense. Why would a burglar take the time to break into his store and not take all the cash? "Have you hired any new employees recently?"

"No one. Everyone has worked here at least a couple of years."

The next morning I stood outside his store and perused the outside of the building. The Bryant Avenue Grocery store was located in the bottom floor of an old apartment building. Customers had to walk down a half flight of stairs to enter. Before I tackled the stairs to meet with Mr. Goldthorpe, I walked around to the side of the building.

Both exterior windows were locked and I couldn't detect any sign of a forced entry. Under each window was a bed of flowers. There was no evidence of them being damaged and I saw no evidence of footprints. I went back to the entrance of the grocery store, carefully walked down the steps, went inside and introduced myself to the owner. "Mr. Goldthorpe, is there any way to enter your store besides the windows on each side and the front and back door?"

"No, those are the only ways that someone could get in."

"Do you give all your employees the combination to the safe?"

"They have nothing to do with this. I trust all of them."

"How come you don't just deposit the cash in the

66

bank every night?"

"We don't lock up until 9:00 p.m., and my bank is closed by then."

"I'm sure they have a drop box for overnight deposits."

"I'm old school. Unless I can give money to a real person, I don't trust putting cash in a box and not getting a receipt. Plus I think it's unsafe to have an employee walk to their car with that much cash."

It was a simple solution, but one he didn't want to consider. It was obvious that this was an inside job, so I offered a suggestion to prove it to him.

"Have you ever heard of ATPR powder?"

"No, what is it?"

I described how we used the powder at the 5th Precinct when we needed visible stain detection. I told Harvey to return to the store right before closing, make sure he used latex gloves and sprinkle a small amount of the powder on the day's currency that was in the safe."

"The powder's dark green appearance is difficult to detect when it's on a dollar bill, but as soon as it becomes moist from the sweat on a person's skin, it changes to a highly visible purple stain. Anyone who touches the money will have the stain on his or her hands for days, and they won't be able to wash it off."

He agreed to give it a try, and I told him that I'd swing back later with the supplies.

Shelley searched the Internet and located a drug store on Nicollet Avenue that sold the powder. I purchased a small amount and also bought a small hand held vacuum.

I returned to Harvey's store to explain the procedure. "You'll need to be careful with this stuff. It can make a mess quickly and you'll be the one with the purple hands."

I showed Harvey how to use it. I wore a pair of latex gloves and sprinkled a small amount on a paper towel.

"Now watch this." I spit on the towel and immediately a large area on the towel turned purple.

"Only sprinkle a small amount," I repeated. "When you open the store in the morning, make sure you use this vacuum to remove the powder off the bills before you touch them.

"Okay," he nodded. "I'll try it the next couple of nights, but if you're asking me, it's a waste of time."

I heard from Harvey the next day and he sounded upset.

"Mr. Goldthorpe, what happened?" I thought that someone must have gotten hurt.

"Patty came to work this morning and her hands were purple. I asked her how that happened, and she said she didn't know, it was like that when she woke up this morning. Is there any other way that her hands could have turned that color?"

"Harvey, listen to me. Was any money missing from the safe when you got in this morning?"

His voice cracked. "$50, but it can't be Patty."

"Has she worked every time money has disappeared?"

"Yes, I checked her schedule, but she's worked for

me for seven years, and I'm godfather to her boy Sean, for chrissake!"

I heard him set the phone down.

"Mr. Goldthorpe, are you there?" I continued to wait until I heard a dial tone.

I called back the next morning and spoke with a carryout boy named Russell. He told me that Mr. Goldthorpe was currently busy, but he promised he'd call back as soon as he had a chance. I never did hear from him by phone, but two days later I received a letter that explained how he had spoken with Patty and they had worked out the problem. Apparently her mother had become ill and even with insurance, the copay for her prescription drugs was more than she could afford. Patty was also struggling and had planned to pay the money back, but never had the chance. Harvey told me to mail him a bill for my time, which I did, and he paid it immediately.

Harvey Goldthorpe treated his employees as if they were members of his family. He was the godfather to Patty's boy, Sean, and that made it difficult for him to accept the truth. Who can say that under similar circumstances, we wouldn't have reacted the same way that Patty did? She was fortunate to have a boss as understanding as Harvey Goldthorpe.

TWELVE

GILBERT ENTERPRISES OCCUPIED the entire 21 stories of an office complex in Golden Valley, Minnesota. Ray Gilbert's personal office was the top floor. On Monday morning I drove to his headquarters, and picked up the file that he had left for me. It included two photos of Marsha Cummings, a copy of her driver's license, the names and phone numbers of two of her friends, and a check made out to the Crow Investigation Service for $10,000. I breathed a sigh of relief, placed the folder in my briefcase and drove into work.

On entering the premises I called to my receptionist. "Shelley, I need to see you for a moment." She followed me to my office and took a seat.

"I'd like you to help me document this information for the Gilbert account."

I opened the folder, spread the files across my desk and we studied what it contained.

Marsha Cummings, the woman that Gilbert wanted me to find, was 28 years old. She was born and raised in

Grand Marais, a small town on the north shore of Lake Superior in Northern Minnesota. After graduating from high school, she moved to Minneapolis and attended four years of college at the University of Minnesota. She worked briefly for a local firm that designed web pages, then took a job at the Gilbert headquarters as a marketing/web page manager and worked there for four years until she quit.

I could see from her employee badge photo that Marsha had Scandinavian features: short wavy blonde hair, pleasant blue eyes and an appealing smile. She was a nice looking woman and it wasn't difficult to see why Gilbert had been attracted to her. The age difference between them stood out: Ray Gilbert was 53 – one of his four children was older than Marsha.

A copy of her job application was in the folder, along with a photocopy of her driver's license, social security number, date of birth and last known address.

Handwritten on a legal pad were phone numbers for two of Marsha's friends. Even though Ray Gilbert had already spoken to both of them, I planned to call them again, in case there was something he had missed. It seemed strange to me that a woman could voluntarily disappear without telling any of her friends where she was going.

I handed the entire file to Shelley and asked that she make a copy of everything, including the check and return the originals to me.

Shelley left my office and I got down to business and mapped out some options that I believed were available for tracking down Marsha. I wanted to start by calling the two friends.

The first contact was a woman named Karen Harley. She answered on the first ring. I explained who I was and the reason for my call.

"I haven't seen nor spoken to Marsha since she moved from Minneapolis."

"Did you even know she was moving?"

"Not at first, but she told me she wasn't renewing her lease at the Calhoun Towers. I had a pretty good idea she was up to something, but I thought that meant she was moving in with her boyfriend."

"Did she tell you the boyfriend's name?"

"No. I knew she was going out with someone because she told me she was busy every time I called her to do something. That's the way Marsha is, so I didn't question it. Everything she did was mysterious."

"Mysterious in what way?"

"I don't know, she was just a secretive person who didn't like to talk about her private life."

"And you haven't heard from her since?"

She didn't hesitate. "No, I haven't, and I'm a little upset. I thought we were better friends than that."

I stayed quiet hoping that she'd say more, but she remained silent. "Can you take my number and give me a call if you hear from her?"

"Hang on." She set the phone down and returned shortly. "Okay, go on."

I gave her my number, thanked her for her time and hung up. Not much help there, so I tried the second number.

"Is this Judy Priestly?"

"Who is this? I'm a little busy right now."

"Is there a better time to reach you?"

"Not unless you tell me what this is about first."

"Marsha Cummings."

"What about her?"

"I've been hired to locate her."

The phone line went quiet.

"Judy, are you still there?"

"Call me back at this same number later on tonight. I should be off work by 6:00 p.m."

After work, I drove home and called Judy from there. She answered after a few rings. "Hold on, I'm driving, let me pull over."

She must have laid her cell phone on the seat next to her, because I could hear the sounds of cars driving by. I waited until she got back on.

"Did that dickhead give you my phone number?" she asked.

"You'll have to be more specific, I know a lot of dickheads."

"Ray Gilbert."

"What makes you think he was the one who gave me your number?"

"Because I know he's been searching for Marsha."

"He said he was looking for her because he was concerned for her welfare."

"That's bullshit," she snorted. "If you believe that, then I've got a bridge in Brooklyn for you to buy."

"Why do you say that?"

"Because I don't trust him. I only had the pleasure to speak with that man a couple of times, but that was enough. I formed my opinion when I was with Marsha on his yacht. As soon as she went to talk to another couple, he tried to hit on me."

"Gilbert? That's surprising."

"I've heard he keeps a harem of women, and I bet he's told them all the same crock of shit that he told Marsha. Only three things are important to him; women, power, and power over women. I'm not surprised that Marsha's hiding."

"Is she? Why do you think she's hiding?"

"Isn't it obvious? Why don't you just leave her alone? If Gilbert is trying to find her, it's not because he's concerned for her welfare. Believe me."

"Maybe I can help. When did you last speak to Marsha?"

"What's your name again?"

"Tony Crow, I'm a private investigator."

"Just what she needs, a pretend cop." She exhaled heavily. "Let me ask you a question."

Not wanting to stop her flow, I let her uninformed description of private detectives slide. "Go ahead."

"What do you really know about Marsha?"

"Only what Gilbert told me, that she was employed by the Gilbert Company, that he and Marsha had an affair, and when Gilbert broke it off, she got upset and quit her job."

"In other words, you know zilch. You're just another

74

one of Gilbert's cronies. Look I haven't talked to Marsha since she moved, and I've had a long day, I'm tired and I want to go home."

Before I could ask another question, she hung up.

I grabbed my legal pad and scribbled a few notes about the conversation.

Priestly's opinion of Gilbert was obviously biased by her friendship with Marsha, but I was surprised to hear the level of negativity she had for him. Besides his recent confession, everything I had previously heard about Gilbert was positive. He was a good family man, religious and gave a decent percent of his income to charity.

Judy had also mentioned that Marsha was hiding, but why would she hide, and from whom? If she had no interest in a relationship with Gilbert, then all she had to do was tell him.

THIRTEEN

WHEN I GOT to work the next morning, I logged onto the St. Paul Credit Bureau to run a report on Marsha. Legally, I wasn't supposed to run a credit report without the written approval of the individual involved, but most people who have had a report pulled on them never know about it or bother to check. I submitted her name, social security number and her last known address in Minneapolis.

The report came up on my computer and I printed a copy for my files. It showed that Marsha Cummings had two current obligations: a college loan and a car loan. On both accounts she was delinquent at least one payment. Two new credit requests had been run in the last year by members of the credit bureau: The Calhoun Beach Towers in Minneapolis, and a software firm in Austin, Texas.

Two accounts were not a lot for someone of Marsha's age; that's when most 28-year-olds were running up their credit limit with the belief that their highest income years still lay ahead of them. But if Judy Priestly believed Gilbert was searching for her, then maybe Marsha also suspected it. If she were hiding, she'd refrain from using her credit card or applying for any type of credit. That would leave a paper trail that could be easily traced. The company that pulled the latest report was MyVoice Software in Austin Texas. It didn't mean that Marsha lived there, but she must have given the idea some thought.

Judy Priestly knew more than she had let on. Not wanting to be cut dead again on the phone, I decided to pay her a visit. Her address was easy to find in the online White Pages. She lived in Bloomington, a south suburb of Minneapolis.

***

I pulled up in front of Judy's one-story stucco house at 8:30 p.m. A red Ford pickup truck was parked in the driveway. A light shone through a partially opened curtain in her front window. Luckily for me, there were only a few steps up to her front door with a railing to lean on. When I rang her doorbell, I could hear it echo inside, and her door opened almost immediately.

"Yes?"

"Judy?" I didn't want to appear threatening, so I stepped back from the doorway. "I'm sorry to bother you, but I was in the neighborhood and I was wondering if I could have a word with you?"

"Who are you?"

"I'm Tony Crow. We spoke this evening about Marsha Cummings."

"Who's at the door?" I heard a man's voice from inside the house.

"Someone asking about Marsha."

"Well, let him in or tell him to go away. I'm trying to watch the football game."

Judy turned back to face me. "You're wasting your time. I've already told you everything I know."

"I understand, but sometimes people forget an important detail. It'll only take a minute and then I'll leave, I promise. I think I've discovered some new information for where Marsha might be living."

"Oh, all right, come in, but you'll have to make it quick, I'm expecting an important phone call." She reluctantly backed away and I took that as a signal that I could enter.

"Have a seat at the dining room table. This is my husband, Jack. Jack this is Tony Crow."

Jack sat on a couch in the living room; he had his back toward me as he watched a flat screen television mounted over the fireplace. Monday night football was on. He waved his hand, but he didn't turn around.

Judy sat across from me at the table. "What's this new information you've uncovered?"

"I believe that Marsha might be living in Austin, Texas. Either that, or she was thinking about moving there."

I watched her expression and she didn't look surprised. "I don't remember her saying anything about Austin."

I was about to ask another question, when her cell

78

phone rang.

"Hold on a second. That might be my call." She grabbed her cell phone out of her purse.

"I can wait," I replied.

She shrugged, answered her phone then walked into the kitchen.

While I waited, I decided to strike up a conversation with her husband. "Who's winning the game?"

Jack turned around. "Vikings, 14-7, but they've been lucky. Both of their touchdowns were a result of their special teams. You might as well make yourself comfortable, if Judy's talking to a friend, she could be a while."

"Thanks. I can wait a little longer, then I'll have to go."

"Do you follow football, Tony?"

"A little but I'm not a hardcore fan."

"I saw you walking with a cane and I thought it might be an old sports injury."

I chuckled. "Hardly."

"Are you a hardcore enough fan to know how many Super Bowls the Packers have won?"

"Well, I know it's more than the Vikings have."

"That goes without saying."

"Why?"

"I made a bet with this guy at work. He's from Wisconsin and I'm sick of him bragging about his Packers, but I think this time I've got him. He claims that Green Bay has won four Super Bowls, but I think it's less than that."

"Nope, sorry, I'm not going to be able to help you with that one."

"I know how we could find out, there's Judy's laptop on the table next to you." He pointed to the computer. "Do one of those search things for me, would you? I'd do it myself, but I'm not computer literate, I can't remember what it's called."

"How about if I Google it for you?"

He snapped his fingers. "That's it."

I opened the cover to the laptop and the screen came to life. I launched the browser and typed in the question about the number of Super Bowls Green Bay had won. As it turned out, Jack was both right and wrong.

"Well, I've got good and bad news for you. The Green Bay Packers have won four AFC/NFC championship games: 1966 and 67, 1996 and 2010, but it wasn't officially called the Super Bowl until 1970. So you may have won the bet, depending on how technical you want to get. If you don't count 1966 and 67, they've only won the actual Super Bowl twice."

"Technical, schmechnical, I'd call that a win, baby!" He yelled and threw a pillow up into the air.

Judy stuck her head in the kitchen doorway and pointed to her cell phone to tell Jack to tone it down.

"Oops, sorry." He went back to watching the game.

"Thanks, Tony. I owe you one."

I was about to close Judy's laptop, when I noticed a mail icon at the bottom of the screen. With Judy still on the phone and Jack more interested in watching the game, I decided to check it out. As quietly as I could I typed Marsha Cummings into the mail application's search bar and found that Judy Priestly had not been telling the truth. She had received seven emails from Marsha in the last three months. I scanned each of them in the preview window.

Six of the emails were just short notes updating her friend on what she had been up to, but one sent in the past week was more interesting.

"Judy, I need a favor. I never forwarded my mail and I'm expecting a check for a tax refund. The person I talked to at the IRS said that it was mailed over two weeks ago. He said he could stop payment on the check and send me another one, but that would take another 3-4 weeks. Could you stop by my last address at the Calhoun Towers and see if the tenant who is currently living there received it by mistake? I still don't have a permanent address, but I arranged with a friend so you can mail it here:

A. Ward

3743 Enfield Boulevard

Austin Texas 78726.

As soon as I find a place to live, I'll let you know.

XOXO

Marsha

I pulled my cell phone from my pocket, took a snapshot of the email, closed the mail application and quietly set the computer back on the table.

"Jack, tell Judy that I appreciate her help, but I really should be going."

"No problem, take it easy and thanks for the help."

I walked out of the house just as he began to scream

at the television set. He was definitely a Vikings fan, and Judy wasn't going to be happy with the noise.

FOURTEEN

I NOW KNEW that Marsha Cummings had applied for a job in Austin and she was having her mail forwarded to her friend who lived there. Before I flew down to check it out, I wanted to see if I could find her friend's phone number in order to call her. It might possibly save me a trip.

Detective Debra Alexander was an old friend of mine from the 5th Precinct. We went out a couple of times after my divorce, but we both could tell that I had not gotten over Amanda. We had remained good friends, and when she visited me at the hospital, she told me to call anytime if I needed her help. I wasn't sure if she really meant it, or if it was just something you tell a sick friend, but I would soon find out. It was too late that night, but I planned to give her a call first thing in the morning.

***

"Debra, it's Tony Crow. How have you been?"

"Great, Tony! Sergeant O'Hara told us about your new private detective business. Everyone here is rooting for you. How's it been going?"

"Good, so far. I've only had a couple of paying clients, but I could use some help with a case I'm currently working on."

"Is there anything I can do?"

"I hope so. I've got a partial name and address for a person I'd like to talk to, but I really need their phone number in Austin, Texas."

"I don't know, Tony, everything is documented now, and to make a request like that, I'd need a police case number."

"I understand, but there must be other ways to find the number." I knew techniques that I had used to get around department rules when I worked there, but I felt uncomfortable suggesting anything to Debra that might get her in trouble. Of course, if she thought of it herself, that was a different story. "It's important," I added.

"I suppose I could include the request with another case I'm working on. Hang on, I'm sitting at the front desk and I need to go back to my office."

She put me on hold before I could reply. A couple of minutes ticked by, then she picked up the phone again. "I wanted a little privacy so I went to my office so we could talk. Give me the information that you have."

I gave her A. Ward's address.

"Just a first initial?"

"Sorry, that's all I have."

"That makes it more difficult, but I'll see what I can do."

I gave her my phone number and she promised to

call me as soon as she discovered anything.

I spent the rest of the day returning calls about my service, reading up on Austin, Texas, and looking into a physical therapy class that had been recommended by my primary care doctor. He felt that exercising in a pool would help me strengthen my legs and allow me to work out without the use of a cane. I found a YMCA branch near my townhouse and wrote down their number. If the trip to Austin turned out to be necessary there was no telling how long I'd be gone, so I decided to give them a call when I returned.

Next I called Don to fill him in about our potential trip.

"I've been thinking about giving my notice at Kelly's anyway," he suggested. "It's only part-time work and I don't want anything to distract from what we're trying to accomplish."

"It's not for sure yet, but if it happens, I'm not going to be able to give you much notice."

"My bags are already packed."

***

The next morning, I received a call from Debra on my way in to work. "You owe me big time. I found the information you want."

"Great, let me pull over and write it down." I stopped by the side of the road and pulled out a pen and paper from my glove compartment.

"Go ahead."

"Her full name is Alison Ward, and by the way it's a new number."

"Okay." I didn't know if that had any significance but I copied down the phone number, and thanked her again.

"Stop by the 5th Precinct some time if you're in the area. We'd all love to hear about your new business."

"I'll do that," I promised.

While I had stopped the car, I decided to call the number that Debra had just given me for Alison Ward.

"Michael?" a woman answered.

"No, this is Tony Crow. Am I speaking to Alison Ward?"

The woman who answered the phone giggled. "Crow, like the bird?"

I joined the fun. "The American crow not the English one."

"Okay." She giggled again.

"Can I speak to Alison Ward?"

"You want to speak with Alison?"

It sounded to me like someone had gotten an early start on the weekend. "Yes I do, who is this?

"Is this a salesman?"

"No, but if this is Alison Ward's phone number, then I'd like to speak with her."

"About what?"

"Marsha Cummings."

"Oh, shit." The phone went dead. I called again and left a message asking that she call me back, but I never heard from her.

I was sure the woman on the phone had to be Marsha Cummings, or someone who knew her. I didn't

86

think she would return my call, but I was positive that Marsha was living in Austin. That meant a trip to Texas for Don and me.

***

The next morning I found Shelley in Don's office helping him unpack some of his things. He had brought in his own ergonomic chair and several books he'd purchased on the makings of a private investigator. What caught my eye were three paintings hanging on the walls.

"Can you believe it? Don painted these," Shelley announced.

I immediately recognized one of the pictures. It was an oil painting of the Mississippi riverbank near Minnehaha falls in south Minneapolis. It was where we'd held keg parties during our senior year in high school.

Don looked up from unpacking his bag. "I painted that from memory when I lived in Hawaii."

"It's good." I stepped closer. "I recall the pit where we used to start a fire when the weather got cold. Which, if I remember correctly, was often. How about this one?" I pointed to a charcoal drawing.

"That's Mount Murresse in northern Mozambique."

I moved to the other side of the room and stood in front of the third painting. He had used a different technique with this one. The colors were brighter and the paintbrush strokes were bolder than the other two. When I stood close to the canvas I had a tough time focusing on the image, but when I took a couple of steps back, it all blended together. It was a self-portrait.

Don nodded and spoke knowledgeably. "That's an early 1900s Post-Impressionist style of painting called Fauvism."

All the images were skillfully crafted, and I was speechless for a moment. "Two questions...who are you and what have you done with my friend Don?"

I went to my office and noticed a message Shelley had taken from Ray Gilbert. I called him back.

"Anything new to report?" he asked.

I told him about the phone calls I made and what I thought they meant.

"That's interesting. I thought Marsha might be in Texas, but I didn't know it would be Austin. Although when I think about it, it makes sense."

"How so?"

"Austin's a big college town with the University of Texas being there, and Marsha always talked about how much she enjoyed her life as a student. She felt a lot less pressure back then." He paused. "What's next? Are you going down there?"

"That's my plan."

"Let me know when you're leaving. My company owns a rental car agency and a hotel chain - I'll take care of that for you. Call my agent as soon as you have the dates set. I'll give him a heads up along with my approval."

He gave me the phone number of his travel agent.

"I also want my assistant to go along," I added.

"That's fine, I'll just need his name."

After I hung up with Gilbert, I called Don into my

office. "What do you know about Austin Texas?" I asked.

"Willie Nelson lives there."

"Maybe we'll run into him." I said. "Ray Gilbert's going to arrange a car and a hotel room. I have some personal things to take care of this weekend, but hopefully we can leave on Monday."

***

That Saturday was Matthew's ninth birthday and I had made plans to take Amanda and him out to dinner. Before my injury I had held a glimmer of hope that Amanda and I could get back together again, but I never got around to bringing up the subject. Now that I was feeling better, I was ready to plant the seed for her to consider that I had changed.

I picked them up at 6:00 p.m. and drove to the Convention Grill on 44th and France Avenue. We were immediately seated in a booth next to the entrance.

"It's been a while since I've eaten here," Amanda remarked.

The restaurant was an old-fashioned style diner with the kind of red vinyl seats that stuck to your bare legs on a hot summer day.

"Your mother and I used to come here before you were even born."

Matt's eyes opened wide as he looked around. "Wow, this place must be really old!"

"I think I even remember what she used to order." I opened the menu to refresh my memory. "If I recall, it was either the homemade chicken noodle soup or a Caesar salad."

Matt crinkled his nose. "It's not one of those restaurants is it?"

"What kind is that?" I asked.

"I've been trying to get him to eat healthy food, but so far he's resisted."

"Well today is your birthday, so if it's all right with your mom…"

"I guess this one time won't hurt," Amanda agreed reluctantly.

"Then I recommend a smoky cheddar cheeseburger, a half order of extra crispy fries and a chocolate banana malt."

"That's what I'm talkin' about!" He made a fist and held it across the table so he could bump it against mine.

I reached into my jacket pocket, pulled out an envelope and handed it to him. "I couldn't decide what to buy you, so this way you can get whatever you want. Happy birthday."

Matthew quickly opened his card. "Cool! A $100 gift card! Thanks, now I can get a couple of new video games."

"Great, that's just what you need," Amanda remarked, but she was smiling.

I ordered for Matt and had the same for myself. Amanda asked for a half order of the Caesar salad with a glass of fresh-squeezed lemonade to drink.

"So how is the Crow Investigation Service coming along?"

I told Amanda about Jo Day and Harvey Goldthorpe, but I didn't mention Ray Gilbert.

90

"I know you, and you have a strong inner drive. You'll be a success as long as you take it easy until you've fully recovered."

I nodded. "I'm going to do my best."

Our waitress brought the food, and like I knew she would, Amanda sampled a handful of Matt's fries.

"Are you just making sure they're not poisoned?" I joked.

Amanda blushed, but she still finished what she had taken.

"I'm going to be out of town for a couple of days, and while I'm gone I was hoping that you and Matt could take care of Max."

Matthew's face brightened up.

Amanda looked at our son. "If we agree, you'll have to make sure that Max is fed and taken for a walk at least twice a day. Is that something you can do? Last time I ended up doing it for you."

"Yes, yes, yes!" he yelled. "When's he coming over?"

"I'll let you know as soon as I book a flight, but right now if we leave on Monday, I'll drop him off tomorrow."

While we finished up our meal, we discussed Matthew's fourth grade teacher at Howe Elementary School.

"Ms. Dailey thinks Matt's going to be a wiz in math. She even named a group after him: Matthew's Group."

"Is that true?" I asked. "Quick, how much is nine plus seven?"

He looked at me like I had gone insane.

"Dad, that's kid stuff."

91

"Sorry," I said. "I guess it's been a while since I was in the fourth grade."

Our waitress came to our table to see if we wanted anything else.

"Dessert anyone?" I asked.

"Nothing for me." Amanda responded and looked at Matthew. "And I think the malt was enough sugar for you today."

"Ahh, Mom."

"Your mother's right," I jumped in not wanting to start an argument.

I was getting ready to leave a tip, when Amanda touched my arm. "Tony, I think that man over there must know you."

I turned around to check it out, but I didn't notice anyone who looked familiar. "Which man?"

"The one by himself in the corner. He's been staring at you, but as soon as you turned around just now, he picked up the menu."

A rugged looking man with a military style haircut and muscular build was sitting by himself. I didn't have a clear view of his face, so I kept my eyes on him thinking that he may look up, but he seemed intent on staring at the menu.

"I don't recognize him," I said, turning back to Amanda. "What makes you think he was looking at me? Maybe it was you he was interested in?"

"Never mind." Amanda must have not liked my comment. She picked up her purse as if she was ready to leave.

I left a tip on the table and stopped to pay the bill as we walked out. Before we got to the car, I stopped. "Amanda...thanks for letting Matt take care of Max. That's one less thing for me to worry about."

"Sure, no problem. He'll enjoy it."

"Did you have a good time?" I asked.

Matthew ran ahead and hopped in the back seat of the car.

"I did, although I can already feel the grease in my stomach from the fries."

"We should do this more often. I think Matt likes it when we're together."

Amanda looked puzzled. "What are you trying to say?"

"I'm talking about us being a family again."

"I don't know, Tony." She tucked her hair behind her ear and looked away. "I wouldn't want to do that just to have it fail all over again. That would be especially hard on all of us. You're no longer a police officer, but being a private detective still means you'll be working at all hours of the night and I'll never know if you're coming home or not."

I tried to hold Amanda's hand, but she pulled it away. "I almost died a few months ago...and, you know, while I was in rehab I had time to do a lot of thinking. You were right to want a divorce, but I've changed since we split and I'd like to give it another try."

She looked away, but not before I could see her eyes were tearing up.

"You don't have to make up your mind now, I just

want you to think about what I'm saying. We could take it slow and see how it goes."

She stepped back. "I'll think about it, but don't get your hopes up. I enjoy living alone with my son and my priority is to make sure he's raised properly."

"I agree. All I'm saying is that it would be easier for you with his father around to help out."

Matthew opened the back window. "Let's get going. I have to get Max's bed ready."

"Let's discuss this another time." Amanda spoke quietly and got in the passenger side of my car.

I understood Amanda's anxiety and if our positions were reversed, I'd probably feel the same way. She was right; putting in the effort and having it fail would be difficult on Matthew and us. But if I would be given another chance, I was determined not to let that happen.

FIFTEEN

I CALLED THE travel agent that Gilbert had given me and booked the flight. It was scheduled to depart at 9:00 a.m. Monday, so I'd have to leave my townhouse by 7:00 a.m. if I was going to pick up Don on the way to the airport.

During the day on Sunday, I dropped off Max, his bed, food, leash and favorite toy at Amanda's. Matthew was already waiting and wanted to take him for a walk. I made sure he had plastic bags in his pocket, and watched as they headed down the street.

We had a non-stop flight that was scheduled to take two hours and forty-five minutes. The attendant at the gate gave us seats in an emergency row exit, which was both good and bad. We could both use the extra legroom, but it was uncomfortable because the seats didn't recline. By the time we had taken off, my back was already screaming for relief.

During the flight we talked about what might happen when I paid a visit to Alison Ward.

"Mostly I think you'll only need to observe," I speculated.

"Why do you think that?"

"I'm not sure. Hopefully I'll get to meet Marsha in person, but so far I've been hitting a dead end trying to reach her by phone."

"Maybe our luck will change."

"Speaking of luck," I said, as I watched our flight attendant walk past. "Does she remind you of anyone?"

Don turned his head. The flight attendant was about our age, 32 give or take a few years, slender with short dark hair.

"Isn't that Cathy Madden?" I stood up to get her attention.

She finished answering a question from a man three rows behind us then turned around.

"Yes?" She turned and stepped toward me. "Tony Crow!"

"Hi Cathy." I sat back down. "I haven't seen you since high school. How have you been?"

"I've been good," she replied. "You haven't changed at all. You still look the same."

"Ahh...excuse me, can I get some service here?" Don had his hand over his face as he jokingly tried to hide his identity.

"Yes, sir, I'll be with you in a minute."

Cathy turned toward me then did a double take. "Don Hanson!" she said a little too loudly. A few people in the next aisle turned to see what the commotion was about.

I knew that Don and Cathy had dated during our senior year in high school, but I didn't realize how serious it had gotten. It was obvious by the looks on both of their faces that they were happy to see each other.

Don stood up and gave Cathy a hug. They quickly forgot about me and talked about what each of them had been up to. Cathy had gotten married to a man she had met in college, and they divorced three years ago. After that, she trained as a flight attendant because she loved flying.

"CLM, will you be laying over in Austin?" Don asked.

She shook her head. "After this stop we're headed directly to LA."

"Well, it was good to see you again and catch up."

"Same here, and it was nice to see you too, Tony." Cathy turned and walked toward first class.

"CLM? What's that?" I asked.

"Her initials: Catherine Linda Madden. It's what I called her when we used to go out. She'd call me DTH."

"Donald Thomas Hanson. You had pet names for each other - that's cute. I think she still kind of likes you."

"Do you blame her? What's not to like?" He smiled and shook his head. "There is one thing that sticks in my mind that happened when I was at her parent's cabin in northern Minnesota."

"What was that?"

"We had only gone out a few times and I was kind of surprised when she asked me to spend the weekend with her."

"Go on."

"Well," Don whispered. "The first night we were getting intimate by the fireplace, and all of a sudden she stopped and wanted to know if I had brought any "safes.""

"Safes?" I asked. "What's that?"

"It threw me off for a moment until I realized that she was talking about condoms. I had never heard them called safes before."

"Me neither, but more importantly, did you have any with you?"

"No, but you can bet I found a 24-hour drug store that sold them."

"I always like a happy ending to a story."

As soon as we got off the plane, I could feel the difference in the weather. Fall had almost arrived in Minneapolis, but in Texas it still felt like the middle of summer. There was more humidity in the air and the temperature had to be at least twenty degrees warmer. I wished I had brought some lighter clothes.

We started walking toward the baggage area, and in the distance I could hear a country and western band mingled with the airport hubbub. We took the elevator down to the baggage area, and above the stairs hung a large banner that read: "Welcome to Austin, Texas, the live music capital of the world."

While we were waiting for our bags, I noticed a man standing against a wall near the claim area, looking in our direction. When he saw me, he turned and walked away. "Hang on a second," I mentioned to Don. I moved

98

off to where the man had been standing. I couldn't tell for sure, because I only got a brief glimpse, but it looked like the same man who Amanda said was staring at me at the Convention Grill.

The crowd around the baggage claim was getting heavy, so I wasn't able to move freely about. It didn't matter anyway - whoever it was had disappeared.

I went back to where I had left Don. He had already picked up our luggage and was standing next to a man holding a sign with our names printed on it. "I'm Tony Crow," I informed him.

"Good afternoon, gentlemen. Your rental car and hotel room have been taken care of. Right this way."

He turned and walked back to the escalator and we followed.

A blue Nissan Maxima was parked on the street in front of the exit. As soon as the driver saw us, he got out and handed me the keys for the car and hotel, as well as his business card. "You're already checked in at the hotel, there's no need to stop at the reception desk. Call me the day before you're going to leave and I'll meet you at the airport and take your car. I've programmed the GPS device, so all you have to do is follow the directions to the hotel. If there is anything else you need help with, just give me a call."

We shook hands and they walked away to a waiting van.

"I could get used to service like that," said Don, throwing his bag into the back seat. I opened the trunk and tossed my luggage inside.

99

Don asked, "Where did you go when we were at the baggage claim?"

"I thought I recognized someone, but he was gone before I had a chance to talk."

We stopped at a Torchy's Taco food trailer on South First, not far from the hotel and brought the food back to our room.

The hotel we were staying at was the Austin Radisson on South Congress Avenue. It was a landmark hotel next to some quirky looking stores that seemed to be doing a brisk business. Our plan was to have lunch, then pay a visit to Alison Ward. I would have felt better if I could have talked to her on the phone first, but she never returned my original message and didn't answer any of my calls.

"I'm hoping that Alison will be sympathetic to our situation," I said to Don. "And put us in touch with Marsha. All I can do after that is explain what Gilbert told me. If she rejects that idea then we'll have to sit outside her house and wait to see if Marsha shows up."

Don nodded. "How do you think I'll be able to help?"

"In case something unexpected happens."

"Like what?"

"Maybe there's a boyfriend involved and he doesn't take kindly to two Yankees coming to Texas lookin' to steal his woman…" I joked. "I don't think anything will happen, but if it does, I'm not sure how seriously a lame man with a cane will be taken."

"I'll be ready for anything."

100

***

Alison Ward lived in a two-story brick home in the Enfield neighborhood of Austin. It was a quiet area with mostly middle-class homes.

We arrived at 4:30 p.m., knocked on the front door, but no one answered. There wasn't an alley or a garage, so she'd have to park in the driveway when she got home.

"Now we wait." I backed the car away from the house and parked down the block. I wanted to make sure I had a clear view of the front door.

Don reached into the backseat and pulled out a small grocery bag.

"Where did that come from?" I asked.

"While you were unpacking, I went to the gas station at the end of the block."

"What did you get?"

"Some supplies that might come in handy while we're doing surveillance. There was a chapter about it in a book I bought."

He pulled out two bananas, a large bag of potato chips, two bottles of water and two empty plastic containers. "Bananas are full of potassium and that means fewer leg cramps when you're sitting in a car for long periods of time." He held up the chips and bottled water. "Potato chips for when you get hungry and the water to stay hydrated."

He gave me one of the plastic containers and smiled. "That's in case you need a bathroom break."

"Hopefully I won't have to wait that long."

"My mother taught me two things that I've tried to remember. Be prepared and wear clean underwear."

"And which of those two things is the container suppose to cover?"

"Maybe both," he grinned as he began to peel a banana.

With my injuries and Don's bulk, neither of us wanted to sit in a mid-size car longer than necessary. We took turns watching the house and getting out to take short walks. Thankfully, at 6:40 p.m., a light-blue Toyota Camry turned into the driveway and a woman got out. I waited in the Maxima until she let herself into the house.

Before Don could get out of the car, I stopped him.

"Why don't you wait here? One strange man at the door is enough, two can be a little menacing."

He shrugged his shoulders. "Okay but I'll have to get out and stretch again."

"Knock yourself out."

I walked to the front door and rang the bell. After a short wait, the same woman opened the inner door, but left the screen door closed. She had shoulder length dark hair, a fair complexion and wore wire-rimmed, oval-shaped glasses. She reminded me of a Sunday school teacher I had in grade school.

"Alison Ward?"

"Who wants to know?"

I pulled a business card from my wallet and held it up to the screen. "My name is Tony Crow. I'm a private investigator and I'm looking for Marsha Cummings."

"You're the same guy who called me the other day."

"Yes, ma'am, I am. Is it possible for me to come in? I have a few questions I'd like to ask."

She looked back over her shoulder, then at me. "How about if I come out there instead?"

"That's fine."

She stepped outside and pulled the door closed behind her. "Why are you bothering me?"

"I'm trying to get ahold of Marsha Cummings."

"What makes you think I know how to get ahold of her?"

"I was told that you're good friends," I paused to see her reaction. "Was that her on the phone when I called the other day?"

She didn't answer; instead she stared over my shoulder toward my car. "Is that your friend?"

I turned around to see Don. Both of his hands were on the hood of the car, his feet were on the pavement and his body was at a 45-degree angle. If I had to guess, I'd say he was stretching his calf muscles. "That's my assistant."

"He's a big man."

I couldn't disagree.

She pulled a pack of cigarettes and a lighter from her pocket. "Hopefully you won't mind if I smoke."

She didn't offer me one or wait for an answer. She appeared to be avoiding eye contact. "You must work for Ray Gilbert?"

I nodded. "He's hired me to locate Marsha Cummings."

She inhaled and blew out the smoke, but remained

silent.

"All he wants to do is speak with her." I paused, not sure how much I wanted to reveal. "From what he told me, he felt bad about the way their relationship ended."

"Yeah, right. Look, Mr. Crow, I'm sure you and your friend," she looked toward Don, "are very nice men, but I don't know where the hell Marsha is."

She took another drag, dropped the cigarette on the cement and put it out with the toe of her shoe. I was getting nowhere fast.

"I appreciate your time, but even if you don't know where she is, I think you know how to get ahold of her. I realize that you don't have a reason to trust me, but before I started my private investigation service, I was a Minneapolis police officer for nine years. I know who Ray Gilbert is, but I'm not his employee. I'm an independent contractor who's been hired to find a missing person, and that's what I intend to do."

She finally looked at me and her shoulders sagged. "How long will you be in town, Mr. Crow?"

"For as long as it takes to find Marsha."

"I know she can't continue to run from Ray Gilbert for the rest of her life." She looked down as she spoke, almost as if she was talking to herself. "You have my cell phone number. Give me a call about this time tomorrow and I'll see what I can do. Maybe there's a way I can set up a meeting."

"Thank you, I'd appreciate that." I turned to go, then stopped. "I'm sorry, we've been waiting in the car for a while, and uh...would you mind if I used your bathroom?"

She frowned slightly, and took a few seconds to process the request. "Go ahead." She opened the door and pointed toward a hallway past the living room. "It's the first doorway on the right."

I was only gone a short time. When I finished, I thanked her and headed back to the car.

"Where did you disappear to?" Don asked when I opened the door.

"I used her bathroom."

"Plastic bottles not good enough for you?"

I stared at the silhouette through the curtain on the front window. I could see someone's shadow, and I wondered if Alison was looking back at me.

"I didn't have to use the bathroom, but I have a feeling that Marsha is staying here. I wanted to check the medicine cabinet."

"Did you find anything?"

"A hairbrush next to the sink. Between the bristles were several short blonde hairs."

"And Alison Ward's hair is dark and long. Was there more than just one brush?"

"I only saw one, but there was another cabinet that I didn't look through. Seeing blonde hair in the hairbrush told me everything I needed to know."

"Maybe she has a boyfriend. Couldn't it be his hair?"

"That's possible, but from the photos that Gilbert gave me, Marsha Cummings' hair was short and blonde."

"If you think she could be living here, why are we

leaving?"

"We're not the police, if she doesn't want to talk, I can't force her, but if I can get her to trust me, we'll have a better chance to hear the truth. I'll call tomorrow like Alison asked me to, and if Marsha still refuses to speak, we'll at least have an idea where she's staying."

I started the car and drove down the block.

"Over there." Don pointed toward a minivan that was parked on the street.

"What?"

"ADC 7185. Remember that."

"Why?"

"The white Chrysler minivan we just drove past. Those two guys pulled up in front of Alison's house while you were talking to her. They've been parked in the same spot watching you ever since."

I slowed down at the corner. Through the rear-view mirror, I could see the vehicle drive off in the opposite direction. I stopped the car, pulled my cell phone from my pocket and repeated the license number into a recording app. "I'll check with the state to find out who owns that car."

Headed back to the hotel, Don asked me to stop. "We just drove past a restaurant. You want to get something to eat? I've heard the barbecue in this town is pretty good."

"Sure." I pulled around the block and parked near the entrance.

The restaurant would have been better off financially if it had closed before we arrived, because of the amount of food Don was about to consume. The first item on the menu was all-you-could-eat barbecue. I wasn't surprised to hear that was what Don ordered.

I had a half chicken, which was plenty of food and I enjoyed it, but by the time I had finished, Don was just warming up. I watched a plate of beef brisket disappear, a rack of ribs and a half chicken, then he devoured the potato salad, coleslaw and baked beans. I knew the end was near when he asked about dessert; either that or he was just slowing down to get his second wind.

While he ate a piece of peach cobbler with whipped cream, I filled him in about Amanda noticing a man watching me at the Convention Grill. I told Don I thought I had seen the same man at the baggage claim at the airport.

Don wiped cream off his mouth with a napkin. "And what about the minivan parked at Alison Ward's house-what do you think it means?"

"There's more going on than just a missing person."

SIXTEEN

WHEN I WOKE up the next morning I had a curious feeling, but I wasn't sure why. There was a thin stream of sun entering under a light-colored window covering next to my bed, and the white walls reminded me of the intensive care ward at the Hennepin County Medical center in Minneapolis. I sat up, turned on the lamp next to my bed, and looked at the clock: 6:00 a.m.

After I had been shot, my physician had prescribed Vicodin to relieve the pain. It was a highly addictive drug that I was only supposed to take every six hours. The exact time I could take another pill was burned into my memory: 6:00 a.m., noon, 6:00 p.m. and midnight. I would often break out in a cold sweat and take deep breaths, watching the clock until the next six hours would pass, and I could get some pain relief.

Stirring into the new day, I recalled a dream that I had during the night. I think it was the reason I remember the drugs. It was similar to other dreams that I had suffered through many nights after the shooting.

***

My collar was turned up, as I walked in the cold rain through Manny Garza's back yard. I followed a busted up sidewalk that curved around the trunk of a large oak tree. There was a carnival at the top of a hill.

In order to get inside, you had to pass through an enormous clown face that formed the carnival entrance. I entered through the clown's mouth to the sound of ear-splitting laughter. Cautiously, I made my way inside and stepped onto a surface that began to undulate, shifting from side to side. I stumbled across the wobbly floor and moved to a room that was filled with mirrors.

I looked to see if anyone else was around when suddenly the lights were turned off, the laughter stopped and I was standing in complete darkness. I didn't move or breathe until a spotlight behind me turned on, and I was staring at the reflection of Manny Garza. He was grinning at me from inside a mirror like a deranged clown.

He was also pointing a gun at my chest.

"Now, do it now!" a voice screamed inside my head. "Pull your gun, shoot Garza and save your partner's life!" But when I searched for my weapon, my hands felt as if they were mired in sludge. Before I could draw my pistol from its holster, four shots rang out.

The laughter from the clown in the entryway started up again, and I closed my eyes because I knew what was coming

When I opened them, the reflection in the mirror had changed. Staring at me with a shattered nose and a disfigured, bloodied face, was Rene Garza. She wept and begged for my help. "Why didn't you shoot him?" she cried.

I felt powerless.

For the third time the reflection in the mirror morphed into someone else. I didn't want to look because I knew what I'd see – my partner, Jeff Lee was standing upright with a hole in his forehead, and another one in his cheekbone. He didn't move but as a thin trickle of blood escaped his lips, I could hear his voice and read the confusion in his eyes: "If you hadn't hesitated, you could've saved my life."

Most police detectives have been affected by some negative experience that occupies their minds and keeps them awake at night. Early in my career I realized that it was important to keep the suffering at a distance, so when attending a particularly grim crime scene, I would try to convince myself that the victim was only a mannequin, similar to the one we used at the Police Academy. But later, when I'd have to break the terrible news to the victim's family, I knew that I'd been deceiving myself, and things were all too real to deny.

Finding the correct words to tell a loved one that a family member has been murdered is excruciating. Their initial reaction would usually be denial. They'd tell me that I have made a horrible mistake, because they had just talked to the victim on the phone, but their denial would change to anguish when they saw the truth in my eyes.

Police officers have the highest suicide rate in the nation, and one of the highest divorce rates. A popular solution is to have a drink as soon as the shift is over. It makes it easier to forget…sometimes.

***

110

I dragged myself out of bed and stumbled into a cold shower, resting my right hand against the wall until my head was clear. The shock to my system felt good, and seemed to momentarily drive my dream and the bad memories away. I finished in the bathroom, got dressed and called Shelley to see if I had any messages. I wrote down the phone numbers and promised I'd return their calls. Before hanging up, Shelley asked when I'd be returning to Minneapolis, but I couldn't give her an answer. All I could do was promise to keep checking in.

My next call was to the Texas State Department of Motor Vehicles. Most states allow a licensed private investigator to look up the owner of a vehicle from a plate number. My P.I. license was from Minnesota, so I suspected Texas would not permit me to do so, but I decided that it was worth a try. Fortunately, the woman who answered the phone took my license number and looked up the owner of the car without question. Texas license plate number ADC 7185 was registered to the Affordable Rental Car Company. That was the same company that provided us with a car and was owned by Ray Gilbert.

Interesting, but was it proof of anything? His car company was the third largest in the United States and must have thousands of cars on the street at any one time. But it did make me wonder if it was merely a coincidence that his company's rental car was waiting in front of the house we were watching.

I returned the messages that Shelley had given me, and called Don in his room. I was feeling uneasy after the dream, so instead of doing anything work related, we decided to explore Austin to see why it was called the music capital of the world. I hoped that it would help alter my mood.

The receptionist at our hotel made a few suggestions: coffee at Flo's across the street, then a leisurely walk along Lake Austin Parkway. The coffee shop turned out to be more of a food trailer, but the coffee tasted great, the people were friendly and even though it was only 10:00 a.m., a young woman was playing her guitar and singing a love song in the vacant lot at the back of the shop.

I decided to get another cup and stay at Flo's and people-watch while Don took a stroll along Lake Austin. My knee was already sore and I didn't want to aggravate it by walking down the long incline to the lake.

In the short time that we'd been in Austin, we could see it was filled with eclectic people. Its motto was "Keep Austin Weird" and it was easy to see why: an abundance of college kids with tattoos and brightly colored hair mixed with 'old hippies,' men and women who had kept their long hair and signature clothing. After devoting most of the 60s and 70s to protesting against war and the powers that be, those 'old hippies' now belonged to the establishment. Most of the people appeared to be happy, which is just what the doctor ordered to turn my mood around.

By the time Don returned, my energy had been restored and I was eager to get to work. I wanted to speak with Marsha and hoped that Alison had been successful in convincing her friend to connect with me. It was earlier than she had requested, but I called Alison Ward from the coffee shop. Don had returned and was seated next to me on a bench.

"Hi Alison, it's Tony Crow. Did you get a chance to speak with Marsha yet?"

"No, no I didn't." She hesitated. "As a matter of fact, I never called her. I'm not accusing you of lying, but I can't take that chance."

"Chance of what? All I want to do is talk with her."

I could hear her breathing, but she didn't reply. "Alison?" I inquired after a few seconds.

"She has too much riding on this."

"Then let me discuss it with her. If she's scared, we won't have to meet in person. I'd be just as happy to talk to her on the phone."

"Do yourself a favor and tell Gilbert that you couldn't find her. I'm sure that won't stop him, but by the time he gets someone else to come down here, maybe she'll have decided to move to another country."

"Don't you think that's a little extreme?"

"Goodbye Mr. Crow. Hopefully you'll do what's best and leave her alone." She hung up.

"That didn't sound too encouraging," Don said as I just looked at my cell phone.

"She won't let me talk to her."

"What do we do now?"

"I think there's a chance that Marsha is living with Alison. Let's park down the block from her house and see what we can find out."

"I'm ready."

"Not right now, I want to spend the rest of the day canvassing the area near Alison's house and showing them pictures of Marsha. It's possible that one of her neighbors has seen her. Tomorrow we can get up early and spend the entire day watching. If Alison Ward won't speak to us then maybe I'll run into Marsha tonight or tomorrow."

I dropped Don at the hotel and drove to Alison Ward's neighborhood. The more I thought about it, the more I believed that Marsha might be living with Alison.

An elderly woman at the end of the same block thought the woman in the picture looked familiar, but after I asked a couple more probing questions, she looked at the picture a second time and wasn't as sure. None of the other neighbors had seen Marsha, and the people who lived on either side of Alison's house, didn't even know Alison's name.

Having come up empty-handed, once again I returned to the hotel, watched a little television, and called it a night. My brain must have stayed active during the night because I had plenty of thoughts about the case by the time the alarm went off in the morning.

I had accepted the job from Ray Gilbert because I believed it was going to be a simple problem to solve: find a missing woman and explain that a former billionaire lover missed her and wanted her back. What man or women wouldn't at least consider that offer? Yet when I called Marsha's friend, she blocked any further contact. Why? What was I missing? The facts as I knew them, were simply not adding up.

Sergeant O'Hara, my former boss at the 5th Precinct used to tell the detectives that if you get bogged down during an investigation, follow the money. In other words, what person or company had the most to gain? Ray Gilbert? He certainly didn't need money, but I wondered why he really hired me.

Because of her financial instability, Josephine Day had been forced to accept the first agency that agreed to work with her. It was the type of work I expected until I could build a reputation and begin to get referrals. The opportunity to work with the lieutenant governor from your home state in only your second month in business was something that most private detectives could only dream about.   I knew I should feel fortunate, but something still made me uneasy.

I called Don to see if he was awake. He said he was, but I suppose that depended on your definition of the term 'awake.' We agreed to meet in the lobby after he had showered and dressed.

For the next hour I immersed myself in the folder that Ray Gilbert had given me. I examined the job application that Marsha Cummings had filled out when she applied for a job at the Gilbert Corporation. She had stated that she had a degree in marketing and experience with creating web pages. That meant she was computer and Internet savvy. Applying for a job at a software firm made sense, but why Austin? Could there be something about this city that would make her want to live here?

There were two pictures of Marsha in the folder. The first photo was her identification badge to wear at work, a typical mug-shot picture, like the booking photos we used to take when a suspect got arrested. The second picture was taken at an outing and showed more of her personality. When I looked at her eyes, it was like they had come alive and were staring back at me. Even though I had looked at this picture before, this time she reminded me of someone.

I gathered up the photos and documents, slid them back in the folder and returned it to my briefcase. I was about to head to the lobby, when the phone rang.

"All set?" It was Don.

"I'm on my way."

I was almost to the door, when something dawned on me. I yanked the file from my briefcase and opened the folder again. This time when I looked at both pictures, I curled my fingers around her head to cover her hair.

"Damn it," I said out loud because it was obvious.

I now realized why the picture of Marsha Cummings looked familiar. We had been talking with her all along.

SEVENTEEN

"INSTEAD OF A restaurant," I suggested as we left the hotel, "let's just get breakfast and eat in the car. I want to get over to Alison's house as soon as possible."

"Both ideas sound good to me."

"You can't be hungry again!" I jibed. "Not after what you ate last night?"

"I was born hungry."

"Sounds like a good title for a Country and Western song."

We bought breakfast burritos and orange juice from the drive-thru at Whataburger. We ate as I drove and I told Don of my theory about Marsha Cummings.

"If that's true, what are we going to do about it?" he asked.

"I'm not sure, but obviously we're not the only one searching for her."

We parked a couple of houses down the street where we could see Alison's Camry in the driveway.

I was about to get out of the car when I noticed

Alison walk out of her house with two large bags. She stuffed both of them in the back seat of her car, and went back to her house.

"What's she doing?" Don asked.

"Let's wait here and see."

Moments later she walked out again. This time she carried a cardboard box.

"It looks like she's moving," Don suggested.

She made two more trips: once carrying a suitcase, and the next time, dragging a large linen bag.

"I'm going to talk to her." I was about to open the car door, when the same Chrysler minivan we had seen yesterday, pulled into her driveway. There were two men inside, but only the passenger got out.

He was a big man, not the size of Don, but no slouch either. He wore a light blue long-sleeved shirt, blue jeans and cowboy boots. He was the closest thing to a real cowboy I had seen so far in Texas.

Alison turned her head as he walked up the driveway. Before she could move away, the cowboy grabbed her from behind and placed one hand over her mouth, the other was around her waist, as he began to drag her toward his vehicle.

Before I could say anything, Don was out of the car. "Let her go!" he yelled as he ran toward them. I got out of the car and hurried as fast as I could manage toward the excitement.

"Stop right there or I'll break her neck." The cowboy's right hand moved down to her throat. Alison's face was red, and it looked as if she was struggling to breathe.

As Don approached, the driver of the minivan backed out of the driveway and drove off.

Instead of walking directly at the cowboy, Don circled him moving to his left. The cowboy moved at the same speed and used Alison as a shield.

Don bounced on his toes. I could hear him say, "Don't do anything you'll regret." His right foot was behind his left; one hand was down by his side and the other was next to his face. He looked like he had been trained in the martial arts.

"I could say the same thing to you. Come any closer and I'll do it."

"Breaking someone's neck isn't as simple as you think, especially when you're also being stalked." Don's voice remained calm, almost as if he was discussing a good restaurant to have lunch with a friend. He took a step toward the cowboy then backed away. Each time he stepped closer, the cowboy lifted Alison off the ground and held her in front of him.

Don paused for a moment to listen. "Good, I think I can hear a police siren in the distance. One of the neighbors must have called them."

The cowboy turned his head for a brief moment and that was all the distraction Don needed. He rushed at the cowboy and this time when he lifted Alison off the ground, Don was ready. He dropped to the pavement with both hands on the cement and swung his hips to the right, like a gymnast on a pommel horse. The lower half of his body acted like a scythe, and his right foot swept

119

underneath Alison's feet and connected with the back of the cowboy's left foot, sweeping it out from under him. With only the right foot to balance on, the cowboy's momentum had nowhere to go but backwards. As he fell, he released Alison before his shoulders and the back of his head struck the cement. She made a soft landing on his chest.

The cowboy's landing was a different matter. On impact, a geyser eruption of air and saliva was forced from his lungs. Then he lay flat on the cement and didn't move.

This all took place before I even reached the driveway. Watching Don in action was both a painful and pleasurable experience. Painful because of what happened to the cowboy, and pleasurable because in all my years in the military and on the police force, I had never witnessed such a large man move so quickly and gracefully. I was in awe.

Alison Ward sat on the unconscious man's chest and appeared to be in shock. Don stood over his victim as if he expected him to get up.

"It looks like you have everything under control," I observed.

He nodded.

"You okay?" I touched Alison's shoulder but she didn't move. "Let's go inside. I think we need to talk."

I helped her up and she swept dirt from her backside and knees. "Do you know who those guys are?" she asked.

"No idea, but I'm pretty sure they're the same men

who were following us last night. Have you seen either one of them before?"

She shook her head and stumbled toward her house.

"Don, why don't you go with her inside and make sure she's okay. I'll wake this guy up and see if I can find out who hired him."

When they were inside, I bent over the cowboy and nudged him with my cane. "Come on, wake up."

He slowly came back to life, and opened one eye. "Is he gone?"

"You missed quite a fight," I said.

He shook his head to free the cobwebs. "Who the fuck was that guy?"

"He likes to be called the Mozambique Marauder or just M&M for short. Now why don't you tell me who hired you before I get him to come back?"

He looked at my cane and sat up. "Now, you I think I could take."

"Don't be so sure about that, I'm pretty handy with this cane, and I'm the guy who taught the Marauder everything he knows."

"Calm down, I was just kidding." He brushed his hair back with his hand and felt the lump in back of his head. "Look, if I thought there was going to be any trouble I'd never have agreed to this."

"What were you supposed to do?"

"Pick up the woman who lives here and bring her to a house in the country."

"Whose house?"

"I have no idea. The guy who was driving the car is

in charge of the details."

Before I could ask another question, the Chrysler minivan pulled up to the end of the driveway and honked. The cowboy stood up, knocked my cane out of my hand, then kicked it across the driveway and ran to the waiting car. I'm not sure there was much I could have done to stop him anyway, but with my cane ten feet away, I didn't even try. I limped to my cane, picked it up and headed to the house.

The front door was open so I walked in. Alison Ward was on the couch clutching a red and black blanket. She had a vacant look in her eyes.

"Where's Don?" I asked.

She nodded toward the kitchen. "He went in there."

"We need to talk," I told her. "I'll be right back."

I went into the kitchen. Don was at the sink drinking a glass of water.

"Where did you learn to do that?" I asked.

"It's called "Tang Soo Do. It's a Korean martial art move that I learned in Africa. Down there you need to protect yourself or you'll never survive."

"A Korean martial art move that you learned in Africa. What will you surprise me with next?"

Don placed his palms together and bowed his head.

"I think bowing your head is actually Japanese, not Korean. But either way, remind me to not make you angry."

I grabbed a glass from the cupboard and filled it with water from the faucet. "Follow me." I turned and walked back to the living room and sat on the couch next to

Alison. Don sat in the chair across from us.

She stared out of the front window as if she were in a trance. "Alison?" I prompted, handing her the water.

After a brief moment, she turned her head and looked at me.

"That's a wig you're wearing isn't it?" I inquired.

She nodded and pulled on a section of the black hair.

"And you're Marsha Cummings."

"How did you know?"

"You always seemed to know what Marsha was thinking, and today when I looked at an old picture of you, it hit me." I paused. "Where were you going?"

"I'm not really sure. I woke up this morning and decided I needed to get out of Dodge. I knew it was only a matter of time before someone saw through my disguise, and it's important that I stay one step ahead of Ray Gilbert." She pulled a tissue from her purse and blew her nose. "What are you going to do now that you know?"

"You don't want to talk to him?"

She shook her head. "Would you? He was the one who sent those thugs to get me."

"Why would he do that?"

"Because of what I know and how I found out."

I was skeptical, but continued, "You know something that's so important that Ray Gilbert tried to abduct you?"

She shrugged her shoulders. "If the press found out what I know, it would end Gilbert's political aspirations, and that's just the half of it. I don't think many people will shop at his store when they know the truth."

"So what are you going to do now?"

"It's time I trusted someone and I don't have many choices." She looked at me. "I'm pretty sure you and your friend just saved my life."

Marsha took several deep breaths then continued.

"Let me clear up something you mentioned on the phone when you thought I was Alison Ward. Ray Gilbert has no interest in rekindling our relationship. That's a lie."

"Okay, I'll buy that for now, so why don't you tell me what the truth is?"

She began by relating how they met and what took place afterwards. "As you know, the man is treated like a god in Minnesota. Not only is he the lieutenant governor, but also his picture is plastered across advertisements in newspapers and on television. Wherever he goes you'll find a crowd following him." She paused and took a drink of water.

"So when a man as wealthy and famous as Ray Gilbert showed an interest in a woman like me, I responded. Even if it had been just for the one night, it was a dream come true."

"Go on."

"It began when he said his wife had canceled a dinner date with him. He told me that he didn't like to eat alone, and wanted to know if I could keep him company. It was all nice and innocent. I had never uttered more than a greeting to him as we passed in a hallway, and then out of the blue he asked me to dinner. I said yes, before he could change his mind. His driver was waiting outside and drove us to a restaurant. I had never ridden in a limousine before and he was so charming."

Marsha confessed how one thing led to another and she ended up spending the night with him in a condominium he owned in Golden Valley. "Everything I was taught told me it was wrong, but it was almost as if I was powerless to stop it."

"I take it that the affair didn't end after that one time."

She shook her head. "No, it didn't. His calls became more frequent and they were always late at night. He was so positive that I wouldn't refuse his invitation that his driver would be waiting outside my apartment before he even called. I later learned that I wasn't the only woman he'd bring to his condo. I heard he called it his Love Shack."

"I knew I was being used, but as hard as I tried not to, I fell in love. It wasn't just with Ray Gilbert, it was also the lifestyle he led. It was an experience that I had only read about in books or seen in the movies. One night he surprised me and said he loved me, but we'd have to wait to get married until he could divorce his wife. Looking back, I can't believe I was that dumb."

She dabbed at her eyes with the tissue. "He called more and more, and I finally brought up his promise to divorce his wife and suddenly the calls stopped. Just like that, no explanation, nothing. I was hysterical and couldn't think straight. He wouldn't return my calls, so I broke into one of his corporate meetings and confronted him. Do you know what that bastard did?"

I shook my head.

"He laughed and called a security guard to have me removed from the building. As I was being led out, I overheard him tell the people at the meeting that cheap labor was getting harder and harder to find. They all laughed."

Marsha quit talking.

"Excuse me," she finally blurted and ran into the bathroom.

"What should we do?" Don asked.

"I'm not sure. Let's wait and listen to the rest of her story first."

"Are you okay?" I yelled toward the bathroom.

"I'm fine, just give me a minute."

"Okay, but I'm a little concerned that our friends might come back."

She finally returned and sat on the couch. She leaned forward, massaged her temples and opened her mouth as if she were yawning. "Sorry, I think I'm getting a migraine."

Don encouraged her, "Is there more?"

She nodded. "There's much more, you've only heard the beginning."

"What did you do after he humiliated you?" I asked.

She looked up at Don then turned toward me. "I tried to get even."

EIGHTEEN

IF MARSHA CUMMINGS' relationship with Ray Gilbert had ended after the humiliation she suffered at his corporate meeting, I might have still believed his version of events. It was possible that Gilbert felt guilty about the way he acted and wanted to apologize, but according to Marsha, that's not what happened.

"Originally I was hired in the marketing department for the Gilbert Corporation, but later I was added to their web design team. I had experience building web pages from a past job and the head of the team preferred to hire someone in-house. I jumped at the chance because it meant that I'd get to learn source code and programming. I always thought that would be important if I ever went into business for myself. Later, I discovered a fringe benefit that I wasn't aware of. Each year the company sent the entire team to a web design seminar and that's where I met Randy Bealman."

"Where does he fit in?" I asked.

"If you were a computer geek," she smiled. "You'd already know that Randy is a legend and considered to be the king of the nerds. In the hacker community he wears a gray hat."

"Gray hat? What's that mean?"

"A black hat hacker is someone who vandalizes or commits theft on other people's networks. They're the ones you hear about on CNN who send you email with a virus attached. A white hat hacker is someone who has been hired by a company to be their network security specialist. That's the guy who is paid a lot of money to build a firewall to protect the corporation's computers from the black hat hacker. A gray hat hacker can be both. In Randy's case, whichever color hat he wore depended on who paid him the most money."

"Why was he at the seminar? I can't imagine the 'king of nerds' learning anything new at one of those."

"He was forced to attend because of a plea bargain agreement he made for breaking into the personal computer of a major corporation's CEO. The way I heard it was that he stole revealing photographs of the CEO's wife and posted them on the Internet. He did it as a joke, but I guess the CEO didn't think it was funny and called the police."

"He must not have much of a sense of humor," Don said sarcastically.

"Randy Bealman knew more about computers than any of the speakers at the seminar could have ever dreamed of. The judge at his trial decided that he should give a talk about the ethics of security management. Randy also thought it would be a good place for him to attend, so he could build his network."

"Anyway, during the breaks, he and I became good friends. He even invited me to his house so I could see his war room," Marsha gushed. "It was unbelievable."

"He had a high back, black-leather chair that was surrounded by three LCD monitors. Each of the screens showed the home page of a corporation that had hired him to design their web page. Unbeknownst to any of them, Randy had installed a 'back door' on their site, so that he could control the content. I don't think he ever did anything destructive; he just liked the power it gave him. The last time I saw him, he told me to call if I ever needed his help."

I nodded, waiting to see where this was headed. "How does he tie into your relationship with Ray Gilbert?"

"You have to understand how angry I was after what Gilbert did to me. I had allowed myself to be hurt and in my mind there was only one way to rid myself of the shame. I wanted revenge."

"And Bealman helped you get that?"

She nodded. "The day after the corporate meeting, I went into work to pick up my personal items from my desk. As far as I was concerned, I had been fired, but I was surprised to discover that I didn't have to be escorted to my desk by a guard, or that the other employees in my group didn't know what had taken place. To them, it was just another day at work."

"Why do you think that was?"

"Gilbert must not have believed I was important enough to fire. I couldn't continue to work for him, but it gave me an idea. That night I went home and gave Randy a call. I disclosed an abbreviated version of what had taken place and explained what I wanted him to help me with. He asked me for some detailed information about the type of setup Ray Gilbert used for the Internet, and then he wrote a program that allowed my computer to mimic Gilbert's hard drive. All I had to do was devise a way to install the program on his personal computer."

I narrowed my eyes. "That can't be easy or every disgruntled employee would do the same thing."

"Actually, it was a breeze for me. I was involved in the company's web page development, so I already knew Gilbert's Wi-Fi security code. He had previously requested that I keep him up-to-date on any changes to the company's page, and he trusted me with the password. By the time he realized what had taken place, it was too late for anyone to react."

"How does a computer virus like that work? Does it allow you to see Gilbert's computer on your screen?"

"No, it's nothing like that, but it did permit me to access his hard drive, and I was able to download his entire disk to my computer. After that I was able to work from my computer and not have to go into his office again."

"My original purpose was to embarrass him by reading his mail, and then to make a list of the women I thought he was sleeping with. When the list was complete, I was going to show it to his wife."

"How did that work out?"

She shrugged her shoulders. "I couldn't be sure that

all the women who sent him email were his lovers, but the number was even larger than I had expected."

"How did his wife react?"

"I never found out. I forgot all about the list as soon as I stumbled upon a private account he had set up."

"Really, that's interesting. Were you able to open it?"

"Not at first, because the account needed a different password than the one I already knew."

"How did you figure it out?"

It would have been easy for me to break into the accounts of most surfers. Believe it or not, the most common passwords that the public uses are: 'password,' 12345 and 123456. With Gilbert it wasn't that easy, I tried every combination of words I could think of: his birthdate, his middle name, the year he was born and his children's names. I eventually ran into a dead end and almost gave up."

"What did it turn out to be?"

"Well," she blushed. "Like a lot of proud males, Gilbert believed his package was a separate entity and gave it its own name. His was named P Rex. Because of our relationship, I knew what it was."

"Similar to Tyrannosaurus Rex?" I asked.

She nodded. "Only with a P instead of a T. When I first typed it in, it didn't work, but then I began to add words that I felt might be successful. It turned out to be the year Gilbert was born. PRex61."

I cleared my throat. "Okay, what did you find out?"

"That Ray Gilbert is an evil and egocentric man. He believes he's smarter and more privileged than the rest of us; a part of me already knew that, but not on this level. The biggest surprise was in a folder that contained information about a secret group he belonged to."

I shook my head. There were probably a lot of secret groups that rich people joined. I was beginning to wonder if Marsha had pushed her revenge motive too far. "I don't understand. How does any of that translate to Gilbert wanting to get rid of you?"

"Well, for starters, his plan is to be the next president of the United States."

"I wasn't aware of that, but why is that unusual? Isn't that a dream of just about every politician?"

"Maybe, but Gilbert has the money and the organization to pull it off. It's his personal beliefs and what he believes is best for the country that should worry you."

"I worry every time someone I didn't vote for gets elected. In the end we're a democracy, and it's the voters who'll decide if a candidate's personal beliefs are what they want." I paused and stared at Marsha. "Obviously I'm not connecting the dots. What am I missing?"

Marsha came right back at me. "To start with, there's Randy Bealman."

"Again? What's his involvement?"

"Randy did me a favor by helping me get revenge against Gilbert, but I should've known he wouldn't do it unless there was something in it for him also. The code he created allowed me to copy Gilbert's hard drive, but it also copied it to Bealman's computer. I didn't realize it at the time, but he received the same information that I did."

"Even the information in his private account?"

She nodded. "As soon as I figured out the password, Randy was also able to access Gilbert's private account."

"Have you talked to him since then? Bealman I mean."

"No, I tried but he's disappeared off the face of the earth. I called him where he worked; I even got in touch with his parole officer. No one's seen or heard from him."

"His roommate's name is Greg Hoffman. Greg told me that Randy had uncovered information about the lieutenant governor that he was going to blackmail him with. His plan was to go to his office, show Gilbert what we had copied from his computer and ask for money to remain quiet. Looking back, Randy would have been smarter to just email Gilbert and explain what he wanted him to do, but with Randy it was also about power. He probably wanted to look into Gilbert's face, but he picked the wrong person to have a pissing match with."

"Why, what happened?"

"The night that Randy went to Gilbert's office, he never returned home. The following day, Greg reported that someone broke into their apartment and removed all the computers and cleaned out Randy's desk. He hasn't been seen or heard from since."

"And you believe that Gilbert is the one who's responsible for his disappearance?"

"It would be quite a coincidence if the two things were unrelated."

We had no proof that what Marsha was telling me

was true, but if it wasn't, she either had a good imagination or was thoroughly paranoid.

"Did you contact Gilbert or his wife after Bealman disappeared?" I asked.

"I never got the chance. I'm sure Gilbert asked Randy where he got the information, and to make his story credible, he must have told Gilbert that we were partners. Shortly after he disappeared, I began to notice strange things wherever I went."

Don looked over at her. "Like what?"

"At first I thought I was being paranoid, but after a couple of close calls, I knew it was real." She paused and cleared her throat. "I saw the same car following me when I was driving, and an official-looking guy in a dark suit was nearby whenever I walked outside. The last straw was when I looked out my bedroom window one night and noticed two men outside my front door. I packed my bags and snuck out the back way. Since then I've changed my name, phone number and address."

Marsha closed her eyes and exhaled; she looked exhausted. "I've been on the run for over a year now, and I've managed to keep my distance from Gilbert until today."

"Has he sent other people to search for you?"

She nodded. "One that I know of for sure, but you're the only person who has discovered the name I was using. Unfortunately that might not be good news for you and your partner."

"Why is that?"

"Because the two men who tried to abduct me must

134

have told Gilbert what took place by now, and if the information I have is as important as I believe it is, your lives are also in danger."

Don and I glanced at each other. "What could be that important?" I asked.

"Instead of trying to explain it, why don't I show it to you instead?"

"You have it here in your house?"

"No. All the information that I downloaded from Gilbert's computer has been saved to a disk. I also made a hard copy and I keep them both in a safe deposit box at my bank."

"Can you take us there?"

"That depends, what do you plan to tell Gilbert?"

"I'm not going to lead you on, it's contingent on the information you say you have. I can't make any promises."

She nodded. "I understand, but I don't know what my other choices are."

Marsha stood up and went into the kitchen. When she returned, she was holding her purse. "You going to drive?"

As we were walking to the car, something occurred to me. "I have a question."

"Go ahead."

"You changed your name from Marsha Cummings to Alison Ward. How easy was it for you to do that? If you live in a rental house, you must have filled out some kind of application."

"I not only filled out an application under the name

Alison Ward, but I applied and received two credit cards under the same name."

"Let me guess," I said. "That had something to do with Randy Bealman."

"Not directly, Randy had disappeared by the time I decided to change my name, but he had already showed me how it was done. It was simple, I broke into the credit bureau's website and added my new name and a social security number to their directory. After that, I just made my payments on time, and no one was the wiser."

Nineteen

MARSHA SAT IN the front seat of the Nissan. Don had squeezed behind her in the back, but from the look on his face he wasn't a happy camper.

"Where are we going?" I started the car.

"The Hill Country Credit Union in Burnet."

"Give me directions, I have no idea where that is."

"I'll program the address into the GPS. That'll be easier than me telling you where to turn."

I pulled away from the front of Marsha's house and headed north on Mo-Pac Highway. I took a quick glance behind me to make sure we weren't being followed and then merged with the traffic.

"Don, watch your side of the car along the highway. I'm still trying to figure out how those two guys knew we were at Marsha's house."

Don spoke while observing at the window. "Were any of them the guy you saw at the grill or the airport?"

"I didn't see the driver clearly, so I can't say for sure, but I don't think it was either one of them."

"So you were being followed even before you knew who I was," Marsha stated. "That's interesting."

"I'm still not sure what to make of it."

As I followed the directions from the GPS device, I pondered Marsha's story. Without having seen any of the evidence, the idea that Ray Gilbert would kill Randy Bealman because he wanted to blackmail him sounded far-fetched, though she might have been right about one point she made - Bealman had never dealt with a man as powerful as Ray Gilbert. The more likely scenario was that he left town because he was afraid of what might happen after Gilbert had threatened him.

It took 45 minutes to drive to Marsha's credit union. The parking lot was almost empty, so I parked in a spot near the entrance. We followed her inside the bank and waited in the lobby while she visited a personal banker. Moments later she reappeared, and was ushered to the far side of the room and through a door that looked more like an entrance to a vault.

She returned holding a manila envelope. "He offered me a booth where we can have some privacy to take a look at this. He said the room was small, but if that's okay, then follow me."

A man waited for us in the hallway then led us to a vacant room. "Just let one of the employees know when you're finished." He held the door open until we were inside.

The banker was right. The room was undersized and would be a tight fit for the three of us. There were no windows and just one light on the ceiling with a small lamp on an undersized desk. With only two wooden chairs to sit on, Don offered to stand. I didn't think we'd be here long, so the size of the room wouldn't be a problem. I sat in a chair next to Marsha and Don stood behind us. "Show us what you've got," I began.

Marsha opened the envelope and spread the contents across the table.

"These are the copies I printed from Gilbert's hard drive. I left the original disk in my safe deposit box. I didn't really understand the information at first, and if it was left up to me I might have forgotten about it and never looked into what it represented, but when Randy disappeared I knew it had to be important and decided to take a closer look."

She picked up a one-page document and handed it to me. "Let's start with this one."

The paper had a list of dates in a column on the right side of the page, and corresponding cities directly across from them. "What's this supposed to signify?" I looked at it and handed the page to Don.

"Meetings Gilbert has attended," she said. "When I first looked at the list, I thought it was Freemason gatherings or something similar to that. You know, kind of a rich, white guys thing. Later I was able to connect the dates to documents and withdrawals he made from his checking account. That's when I began to understand the true significance of the group."

"What kind of group is it?"

"I think you'll see for yourself before long."

She shuffled through a couple of papers, then

handed me another document. "I downloaded this one off the Internet."

Don looked over my shoulder as I read it. It was a New York Times article that was written in 1967 about Ray Gilbert's father, Preston Gilbert. The story was about entrepreneurs and how they added to their already enormous wealth by investing in German banks before the start of WWII.

I was already aware of the large amounts of money some investors made off the pre-WWII German economy, but I wasn't aware that one of them was Gilbert's father. "Germany suffered through a major economic depression after World War I," I explained. "Adolf Hitler grew in popularity by building highways and infrastructure to create jobs, but he needed outside investors to help with a cash infusion. I'm not trying to vouch for Preston Gilbert, but there wasn't any way that he could have known the atrocities that Hitler would later perform against the Jews."

Marsha acknowledged my comments, but had more to add. "I understand that, but even before Germany invaded Austria, Hitler's beliefs were well known and documented. I think you'll see that this was just the beginning of a pattern for the Gilbert family. The United States government forced most of the investors to pull their money out after World War II began, but right after Germany surrendered, some incidents the elder Gilbert was involved in are questionable."

She handed me another document.

"What am I supposed to be looking for on this one?"

140

I asked.

"It's a history of the Gilbert store with a detailed list of corporate executives that were hired after Germany's final surrender on May 8, 1945."

I silently read the names of the Gilbert Corporate executives, but none of them held any significance for me.

Marsha stood up. "Have you ever heard of these three men?" She bent over and pointed.

The first two names didn't ring a bell, but the third one sounded familiar. "Wasn't this man a leader of a white-supremacist group in the United States at one time?"

She nodded. "And these two were German officers who fought against the allies right up until the war ended."

That took me by surprise. "Two former German officers were hired by the Gilbert Corporation? That can't be possible."

"Not just hired, they were members of his board of directors."

"That's outrageous. There had to have been a law against a U.S. corporation hiring former members of the German military."

"There was, but it wasn't universally enforced." Marsha pulled another document from the file and handed it to me. "Politicians are a lot like puppies – they learn when they're rewarded. In this case, the politicians learned to look the other way when a large donation to their campaign was included."

On the paper were listed two substantial donations to politicians that were made immediately before the two German officers were added to the Gilbert Corporation board of directors.

"Gilbert's father was involved with this?" I asked.

"Yes, and now Ray Gilbert is following in his father's footstep. Besides hiring ex-Nazi's, he's a firm believer in some of the same principles including eugenics."

"Are we speaking about the same man? Ray Gilbert, the CEO of the Gilbert Store chain?" I couldn't wrap my mind around that idea, but then when I thought about it – he had shown me his Nazi war memorabilia at his house, and displayed an unusual interest, offering to show me more of his collection. At the time the thought of looking at the antiques and what they represented disgusted me; although I did wonder why he'd think that I had an interest.

"The final answer, as he calls it," Marsha disclosed, "is to be elected president of the United States. The voters will have the final say if Ray Gilbert is elected, but they won't be allowed to see the real man and what his actual beliefs are before the election."

"The final answer?" I repeated. "That's similar to Hitler's final solution. You have proof of that?"

"It's all there, you can read it for yourself." She pointed to the folder then looked at her watch. "Take your time, I have all day."

Marsha stood up and Don replaced her in the chair. We split up the information and read while she answered questions. The files included Ray Gilbert's personal files, emails, bank records, political donations and lectures, and articles on the philosophies of men who believed in white supremacy. Marsha said that all the information had been copied from Gilbert's hard drive. To get a better understanding of what we were looking at, it would have been helpful to hear his point of view, but I knew that wasn't going to happen.

The evidence Marsha had collected was compelling and would have made a great novel. I was barely able to pull my eyes away until I had finished reading the last document.

Ray Gilbert, a hero in the eyes of many people, was a leader in a white-supremacist group in the United States. He had donated large amounts of money to parent groups that were nothing more than a front for human sterilization. Was that possible?

My better judgment told me it couldn't be true, but the information she had shown us was overwhelming. And I had also witnessed the two men trying to abduct Marsha.

When we had finished looking at the last file, Marsha gathered the documents off the table and pushed them back into the folder. "Take these, they're yours," she handed me the folder.

"What are you going to do with the original disk?"

"I haven't made up my mind yet."

"How about you?" Don gestured to Marsha. "What are you going to do?"

"That depends on what you decide. If you leave it up to me, I'll go somewhere a long way from here, and I'm not just referring to Texas."

"One thing I'm sure of, is that I can't sit in this chair any longer." I stood up and stretched my back. "Let's get some coffee and we can discuss our options."

We walked down the hall, through the lobby of the bank and toward the main entrance. Just before opening the door to leave, I noticed a red Ford Explorer, parked directly across the lot. There were two men sitting in the front seat, and I was sure one of them was the guy that Don had dropped in Marsha's driveway.

"Hold it." I reached over to stop them from walking out. "I think we've been followed. Wait here."

I turned and headed back to talk to one of the bankers.

"Is there a way out of here, besides leaving through the front door?"

The banker looked concerned. "Is something wrong, sir?"

I smiled and spoke discreetly, "No, it's just that an acquaintance of our friend is outside, and we'd rather not be seen with her."

He turned and pointed to the far side of the lobby. "See the restroom sign hanging from the ceiling?"

"I see it."

"Walk past the sign and continue down the hall, until you get to the exit. You can leave there, but you'll have to walk around the building to get back to the parking lot."

"Thank you."

I went back and looked outside again. I wanted to see if the Ford was still there. It was.

The three of us leaving together didn't seem like a good plan. We'd be too easy to contain, but I had another idea. "Marsha and I will leave and walk casually to our car. That way we'll find out if they're going to confront us here, or they only want to know where we're going."

I informed Don of the back exit and what I wanted him to do. "You go out that way and watch from the back of the building. If they get out of their car, come up behind them."

Don saluted as he walked away.

I turned toward Marsha. "Stay behind me and don't look at the Ford as we're leaving."

As soon as we walked outside, I heard a car door slam. I didn't turn around until I felt a hand on my shoulder.

"Going somewhere Hot Shot?"

It was the cowboy. Standing next to him was another man with a military haircut; he wore sunglasses and was formally dressed with a blue sport jacket and gray pants. It was the same man I had seen at the restaurant and the airport.

The cowboy had grown in confidence since I last saw him. "Well, well," he remarked. "What do we have here?"

"I almost didn't recognize you," I smiled sweetly. "If I remember correctly, you were running away with your tail between your legs."

He let go of my shoulder and balled his fist.

"Leonard, not here," the man with the sunglasses ordered.

145

"Where's your buddy?" The cowboy pressed me. "He won't be able to cheap shot me like he did the last time."

"Leonard," I smiled. "That's hilarious. You're a tough guy as long as you have someone to back you up."

The man with the sunglasses stepped between us and pushed the cowboy away. "Take them over there." He pointed toward the side of the bank next to a carwash. That wasn't a good sign. Whatever their plan was, they didn't want to be seen. "Do as I say and no one will get hurt."

He pulled his jacket away from his shirt so I could see a black nylon holster under his right shoulder. It was holding a Glock pistol. "I don't want to cause a scene, but I will if I have to." His voice remained calm. "Give me your briefcase."

He reached out to take it, but I held it tightly under my arm.

"Instead of fighting, why don't you give me your address – we'll drive over and we can discuss the contents of the briefcase over a chilled bottle of Chablis."

He hit me with a blow to my right side–it took me by surprise–just above the belt line, and where I had been shot. It wasn't a vicious hit, but it was well placed. I struggled to breathe and hold onto consciousness.

"I'm not fooling around!" he barked and took a step back.

The cowboy also wanted part of the action. "He thinks he's funny. Leave him with me and I'll give him something to laugh about."

While I was hunched over, Marsha made eye contact. Her face was pale, her eyes were wide and it was obvious that she was terrified. I nodded because I was out of breath and couldn't speak. I was trying to show her that everything was going to be all right, but I wasn't feeling that way.

"Let's try this again. Give me your briefcase."

This time I didn't resist. "What are you going to do, shoot us in public?" I gasped between breaths. I had hoped that Don was watching and would call the police. I quickly realized otherwise when I heard a voice from the back of the building. I hadn't given this group enough credit – I didn't think they'd be carrying weapons or have someone waiting behind the bank.

"Look what I found." A third man walked out holding a gun firmly between Don's shoulder blades. "Anybody know this guy?"

Don walked calmly as he was being pushed forward. The cowboy sauntered over to him and you could almost smell the testosterone in the air. He smiled and spat in Don's face, but Don simply yawned as if nothing had happened.

"We're here to do a job." The man in sunglasses pushed the cowboy away. "Fucking amateurs."

Don and Marsha were handcuffed behind their backs by a single-loop, plastic pull-thru device. They handcuffed me with my hands in front so I could hold my cane to walk.

A couple walked by from a nearby store. I tried to make eye contact with the woman, but for all she knew I was a criminal being arrested for robbing the credit union. They walked past us and kept their heads down.

Don and I were shoved in the back of the Ford while the cowboy drove.

Marsha rode in the front seat of the minivan with the other two men. It was obvious by the way they carried themselves that they were professionals, possibly even retired military or FBI agents. Because they were both with Marsha, it was clear that they believed she was the important one. I still wasn't sure where the cowboy fit in.

As we drove north of the city of Burnet, Don and I exchanged glances as he turned slightly to show me his hands. He was attempting to cut through the plastic handcuffs by rubbing them across a metal piece on the back of his belt. With the tight restrictions of the backseat, I thought it would be difficult for him to get enough leverage.

"Hey Leonard, do you know where you're going?" I asked.

He turned his head slightly, as if to answer, but thought better of it and continued to drive.

We passed a municipal airport on highway 281 and made our way through the city of Lampasas. I was searching for familiar landmarks in case I had to relate to the police where we were taken, but I could've been in Africa for all I knew about Texas. Nothing looked familiar.

The driver in the minivan stayed in contact with the cowboy by cell phone. I tried to listen to their conversation, but it was impossible to hear clearly from the backseat. It sounded as if the cowboy was giving directions. Maybe he had been hired because of his knowledge of the area, but I felt he was the weak link of the three, and someone we could take advantage of, if given the opportunity.

The long drive gave me time to think about our situation. When I was a police officer, I was trained to track a suspect and, in turn, to recognize when I was being followed. It hadn't occurred to me that anyone would be trailing me at the Convention Grill or the airport, and I was disappointed that I had let my guard down. However, at Marsha's house and again at the bank, I had been looking for suspicious activity but hadn't detected any. The logical explanation was that someone had placed a GPS device on our rental car…and that someone had to be Ray Gilbert. That would explain why he offered to arrange a car for us through his travel agency, and most likely our hotel rooms were also being monitored.

A more immediate concern was our current situation. While it was possible that the three men only wanted to question Marsha and remove any incriminating evidence against Gilbert, I wasn't counting on it. We had seen their faces and I knew the cowboy's first name, therefore I couldn't depend on them letting us go. I had to figure a way out of this mess, and fast.

***

After about an hour of driving, we finally pulled off the highway onto a gravel lot. The only visible building was an old farmhouse with an outbuilding about a mile

149

down the road. "Get out, pretty boys," the cowboy ordered, opening our door.

We waited outside the car until the minivan arrived. The three of us were escorted along an inclining dirt path until we came to a rusty metal warehouse that was hidden behind a row of trees. The odds of being rescued in such a secluded area were not good.

When we entered the building, the guy in the sunglasses directed the cowboy and us men into a room across from the entrance. "Watch them and we'll be back as soon as we're finished with her." He continued down the hall with Marsha.

Our room smelled damp, as if the plumbing had recently backed up. The cement floor was old and cracked; the walls and light fixtures were covered with dust. It appeared to be an old warehouse that hadn't been used in a while. The cowboy found two metal folding chairs in a closet and set them in front of an old metal desk.

"Make yourselves comfortable," he drawled, taking a seat behind the desk and placing his revolver in a drawer.

He dragged his cellphone out of the front pocket of his pants. "I'm going to check my mail. I'll get to you two in a minute, but first I have to check in with the ladies." He stared at his phone then stuck it back in his pocket. "It looks like the girls are going to have to wait. I can't get a signal in this dump."

While the cowboy had been preoccupied with his cellphone, Don had moved his chair closer to the wall. From that angle, I could see that he had continued what

150

he had started in the car. He was rubbing the plastic handcuff across a sharp piece of metal on the back of his belt. It looked like he was making progress, but it was going slowly.

"So, Cowboy, what do you want to be when you grow up?" I asked.

He turned toward me and frowned. "Shut the fuck up. I'm trying to think."

"I wouldn't want to interrupt a major event like that," I bantered, trying to keep him distracted.

He ignored me and pulled a jackknife from his pocket, threw his feet up on the desk and began to clean his fingernails.

After about thirty minutes of watching the cowboy manicure his nails, my spine and knee were screaming for relief. "Any idea how long this is going to take?" I asked.

"Why, is there somewhere you have to be?" He turned toward me and smirked. "Make yourself comfortable, you won't be going anywhere for a while. You've made an enemy of a very important person."

Suddenly the cowboy turned and looked at Don. "Hey, what the fuck do you think you're doing?"

He stood up, grabbed his gun and walked over to investigate. Instead of hiding his activities, I was surprised to see Don move his head from the wall and show his hands. But as the cowboy moved closer to take a better look, Don blasted off his chair and butted him in the face. The cowboy's nose exploded, and his cheekbones and mouth caved into his skull. He took one step back before his legs crumpled beneath him and his gun slid across the floor.

Don's forehead was covered with blood, but I doubt any of it was his. He sat on the floor, slid his hands underneath his backside then wiggled them past his knees and under his feet. With his hands in front of him, he was able to use his strength to tear through the rest of the plastic.

"That worked out well," I said in a low voice. "You had me worried for a minute. I didn't understand what you were doing."

"It was taking too long trying to cut through the plastic because I couldn't see my hands," Don explained. "I was hoping he'd look over my shoulder to see what I was up to."

"Okay, get me out of these handcuffs," I urged. "His jackknife is on the desk."

Don retrieved the jackknife then used it to cut off my handcuffs. I bent over and picked up the gun, then checked the cowboy's pulse. It was weak, but he'd be fine - though he'd need a good cosmetic surgeon before any of his girlfriends would return his calls.

"That should keep him quiet for a while," I said. Check his pockets. He must have the keys to the Ford in there."

Don found the keys and went to look for Marsha. We turned right and snuck down a hallway, until we arrived at the only other room that had a door. I motioned to Don to keep quiet and put my ear against the door. Silence.

I shook my head to let Don know I couldn't hear

anything and lightly turned the doorknob. Don nodded. If Marsha was still here, I wanted our entrance to be a surprise. I set my cane against the outside wall, braced myself and pushed on the door. It swung open as I stepped inside with both hands on the revolver.

"Freeze!" I yelled.

Besides Marsha, there was only one man in the room, and he was sitting with his back toward us. "Drop your gun!" I pointed the revolver at the back of his head. He froze for a second then he removed his gun from the holster, bent over and set it on the floor, between his feet.

Marsha was sitting in a chair next to him with her hands behind her back. "Thank God," she exclaimed. "The other guy left about ten minutes ago. He couldn't get a signal on his cell phone, so he's driven to higher ground about a mile away. He could be back any time now."

"Okay, let's get you out of here."

Don took the jackknife and cut through the plastic around Marsha's hands.

"What should we do with him?" I pointed to the guy who had been guarding Marsha.

"I'll lock him in there." Don pointed to a closet. "No one will hear him."

Don pushed him into the closet and for good measure brought the handle of the jackknife down on his head. It must have been effective, because I heard his body hit the floor. Just to be sure, Don wedged a metal chair underneath the doorknob. "That should hold him for a while. Let's go see if the minivan has returned."

We hurried to the door where we had entered. I opened it and peeked outside. The Ford was there but the minivan was not. I hobbled to the car, Marsha got in the backseat and this time Don drove.

"What happened in there?" I asked Marsha. "What were they trying to find out?"

"They wanted to know if there were any other copies of the files, and how much you knew. I told them that you had the only one, but there hadn't been enough time for you to look at it."

"Do you think they believed you?"

"At first, I don't think they did. They made a bunch of threats and told me what they were going to do, if I didn't tell them the truth, but I stuck to my story."

"You're tough," Don praised her.

"I really didn't have much of a choice. I knew they weren't going to let us go, no matter what I told them."

"Are you sure of that?" I asked.

"Positive. You saved my life, again."

"Then I'm glad we showed up when we did."

While Don drove I divulged my theory about a GPS device on our car. "That makes sense," Don acknowledged. "Maybe we should rent another car and get a room at a different hotel."

I thought about Don's suggestion, and he was right, but first I wanted to find out if my theory was correct.

"Let's stop at Marsha's credit union so I can check the Maxima. We'll leave the car there, but I want to find out how they knew where we were going. I still need proof that Gilbert is behind this, and finding a bug on the rental car would be a start."

Marsha spoke with great assurance. "I already have all the proof I need."

"I understand," I said. "If he's a white supremacist like you believe, and has plans is to run for President and change the way we live, then I won't sit by and do nothing. But if for some reason you're wrong, the information you publicize could ruin a man's life and career."

"You can't deny what just happened to us, can you?"

"No, someone is responsible, but I have to be certain it was Gilbert."

Marsha shook her head. "Go ahead and do what you have to do, but it's a waste of time."

As Don drove, I stared out of the side window and thought about a plan. For my reputation as a private investigator, I needed to be positive that Gilbert was responsible otherwise I'd look like a fool trying to take down the lieutenant governor.

"I'll call Gilbert and fabricate a story," I detailed. "I'll tell him that I set up a meeting with you and if his goons show up, then I'll know he's accountable." I turned toward Marsha. "Do you have a place you can stay and hide out for a while?"

"No, not really. I can't go back to my house now that Gilbert knows where I live."

"He knows the name you were using, so you can't use your credit cards either."

I didn't use my credit card for the same reason. It might alert Gilbert that we were on to him and had

155

moved from his hotel. I didn't want that to happen until after I called him. "I have enough cash to pay for two rooms at another hotel, but just barely. Don and I might have to share a double."

Don glanced at me smiling. "You don't snore do you?"

"If I do, just pretend it's a sound machine and you're listening to an ocean breeze."

"Just as long as it's an ocean breeze and not a tsunami."

Marsha smiled. "Thanks, Tony. I appreciate the offer."

Don drove to the Burnet Credit Union and parked the Ford next to our rental car. I got out and immediately began to search the Maxima for a GPS device. I looked under the hood, the front bumper, under the grill, in the trunk and the windshield washer holder, but I came up empty. Another common location to hide it was underneath the car. I got on my back, crawled underneath and looked under the rocker panel, the exhaust system and the frame, but I still didn't find anything. Either someone was better at hiding 'bugs' than I was at finding them or I was wrong about how they knew where we were going.

Even though I didn't find any bugs, it seemed prudent to find another hotel and rental car. I still wasn't convinced that Gilbert was responsible for what happened to Marsha, but I couldn't take the chance that he was. We spent the rest of the afternoon finding a new hotel, and I leased a Chevrolet Tahoe. We abandoned the

Explorer in a vacant lot. Marsha stayed in her room, and Don and I decided we needed some coffee. We drove the Tahoe to a Starbucks so we could talk.

I ordered coffee for both of us and we sat at a table next to the window. I took my cell phone but the battery was dead. "The battery on this thing is running down awfully fast lately. I think it might be time to get a new phone."

Don spoke before sipping his coffee. "What are you planning to do about Gilbert?"

"I'm going to explain that I'm checking in to update him on what happened."

"You think he'll buy it?"

I shrugged my shoulders. "I'll try to be convincing, but if not, we're no worse off than we are now."

"And if it is Gilbert, what can we do about it?"

"I haven't decided yet, but I have some ideas. Hang on a second, I'm going next door to the bookstore."

"All of a sudden you thought of a book you wanted to buy?"

"No, I need a map."

I returned shortly with a street map of Austin. If I was going to call Gilbert and tell him about a meeting with Marsha, I'd have to give him a location. I spread the map on the table. "Trailhead Park in northwest Austin might be a good spot to tell him where we're meeting. I'll drive by first before I give him a call. If it looks promising, I'll tell him the meeting will be at noon tomorrow. I'll pick up a pair of binoculars tonight, and we'll get there early in the morning to find a spot where we can watch."

After we finished the coffee, we walked out to the car and I plugged my phone into the adapter in the cigarette lighter. Even though the battery had been running down quickly, it seemed to charge up at the normal speed, which was good because I needed it to call Gilbert.

I typed in the address of the park into the GPS device on the car and followed the directions. Trailhead Park was smaller than I thought it would be from the map, but we located a hill in a residential section just north of the park; from there we'd have a view of the surrounding area and parking lot.

On the way back to the hotel, I located an REI store and purchased a pair of compact binoculars with a magnification power of seven. That would be strong enough for what I wanted it to do. While I was there I also bought another briefcase to replace the last one that had been grabbed by Marsha's abductors.

I drove back to our hotel and after I had parked, I told Don that I needed the room so I could call Gilbert. "That's fine," he complied. "It looks like a nice evening, I'll take a walk. I noticed a restaurant a ways back, and if the stars are aligned correctly maybe I'll meet a lonely young lady and we'll share a taco. I'll see you tonight, roomy."

He got out of the car and walked away singing *Some Enchanted Evening*, from the movie *South Pacific*.

***

If Gilbert had been responsible for hiring the men who abducted us, then he already knew what had taken

158

place at Marsha's house and the credit union. What he couldn't be sure of was how much I knew. I needed to play off that doubt and convince him that I was still onboard with getting Marsha to speak with him. But I would have to convince him that I was upset.

I waited until my cell phone was fully charged and called Gilbert. I had expected it to go to his voicemail, but he surprised me and answered on the first ring.

"Tony?" He sounded confused when he answered. "I guess I wasn't expecting to hear from you."

"Mr. Gilbert," I began, "I think you owe me an explanation."

"For what?"

"About Marsha Cummings. You told me the reason I was looking for her was that you wanted to get back with her again. She told me an entirely different story."

"What I told you was true, I want to see her again so I can apologize. What I did to her was wrong. I acted irresponsibly and humiliated her at a meeting and I regret it. I couldn't tell you everything that happened when you were at my house because my wife was present."

I decided to go ahead and tell my version of what had transpired to test his reaction. "Are you aware of what's been happening down here?"

"No, I'm not, have you found Marsha yet?"

I gave him a run down of our ordeal. When I finished, I had to wait for his reply.

"What on earth?" he exclaimed then fell silent.

"Three men were involved. You're saying that they

159

don't work for you?"

"They do not!" he said forcefully. "This is the first I've heard of it."

"But you were aware that Marsha downloaded information off your hard drive."

He didn't answer right away. "Yes," he finally admitted. "I knew about that. She was angry with the way that I acted and I don't blame her, but what she downloaded is worthless to anyone besides myself."

"Why is that? She thinks it might be important."

"Did she say why?"

"No. We were heading to a coffee shop to talk about it and that's when we were grabbed by three men."

"I'm sure she was going to tell you about the email."

"What email?"

"I'll be the first to admit that I haven't always been faithful to Gloria, and I'm afraid that some of my past indiscretions are documented there."

"You're telling me that she was going to show me letters from other women?"

"Yes, I'm afraid that's right. Do you know where she is now? I'd like to speak with her and explain."

"After we escaped from the warehouse yesterday, I dropped her off at her car, and we went our separate ways. This morning she called me."

"What did she want?"

"She asked to meet so she can turn over the information from your computer. I'm not sure I want to get involved, especially if it's only a list of women. I was almost killed once and I don't want to go through that again for something so trivial."

"Maybe Marsha believes it's something more than it really is," he hesitated. "I know she wants to hurt me, but I'd appreciate it if you could meet with her and see what she has to say. I'll pay you double for your time."

"And you had nothing to do with the abduction?"

"It's the first I heard about it."

"I'll take you at your word."

"Thank you, Tony. Where are you going to meet?"

"At Trailhead Park in northwest Austin at noon tomorrow. Do you want me to say that you're still interested in getting back with her?"

"Yes, nothing's changed. I know she's confused and she probably detests me, but I miss her and I'm looking forward to seeing her again."

"I'll give you a call after the meeting."

I had to admit that Gilbert almost convinced me, but I had to remember that he was a politician with a lot of practice in stretching the truth.

TWENTY

I WOKE UP early the next morning, got dressed and told Don that I'd meet him outside as soon as he was ready. I went next door to see if Marsha was up, but I couldn't hear any noise inside her room, so I didn't knock.

It was going to be another warm day in Austin with the temperature expected to be in the mid-90s, but after breathing refrigerated air from the hotel air-conditioning unit during the night, my lungs felt refreshed.

I hadn't spoken to Amanda since I'd left for Austin. Normally I'd call her every two weeks to verify that I was picking up Matthew for the weekend. With the two of them taking care of Max, and me having told her about wanting to get back together again, I felt like I should stay in touch more often. It was Saturday morning, so there was a good chance that both of them would be home.

"Amanda, it's Tony. How are things going?"

"Good. Are you back in town?"

162

"No, I'm still in Austin, but hopefully not for a lot longer. How have Max and Matt been getting along?"

"Matt's been more responsible than the last time Max paid us a visit. He takes him for a walk first thing every morning before he leaves for school, and another one as soon as he gets home. He even feeds him twice a day. The bad news is that they're bonding, and he's going to be sad when you have to pick him up."

"From the sound of it," I said, "Max might not be too thrilled about it either."

Amanda's voice sounded cheerful, but that might not have had anything to do with me. Then a thought struck me – I wasn't even sure they were alone. Suddenly I felt a little silly.

"The two of them have been inseparable. I've even been thinking that maybe Matt's old enough to have his own dog. Sometimes I think he's lonely."

"Well, I can drive him to a couple of animal shelters in the area as soon as I get back. There must be a lot of rescue dogs that would appreciate a good home. That way he could pick out the dog he wants."

"That's a good idea, but can we talk about it later? You called just as I was headed out the door."

"Hey, Dad!" I heard Matthew yell in the background.

"Okay, I'll give you a call when I'm back in town. Tell Matt I'm thinking about him."

"I'll do that, and Tony?"

"Yes?"

"I've been thinking about what you said, but it's going to take time. Why don't we take it slow and see

163

what happens."

"That's all I'm asking."

Talking to Amanda brought my spirits up; though I had to remind myself that I wasn't her husband and I no longer had a right to ask if she was alone. But that didn't mean I didn't want to.

I walked down the block to do some window shopping, stopped at a grocery store and bought a couple of local magazines to read until Don was ready. I knew he'd be hungry so I stopped and knocked on Marsha's door. She answered and I asked if she wanted to go with us to have breakfast.

"I just got out of the shower. I can be ready in about twenty minutes."

"No, hurry, just pound on our door when you're ready to go."

***

We ended up at the Kerby Lane Café. Don ordered a breakfast platter with a double order of bacon. I asked for a breakfast quesadilla with a glass of fresh squeezed orange juice and Marsha had a ham omelet. We talked while we waited for the order. "I never notice it much when I'm at home, but now that we have to go out to eat for every meal, I realize how much food we consume every day."

Don nodded. "I think about that a lot, and if it was up to me, I'd add at least one more meal to round out the day."

"Besides breakfast, lunch and dinner? What are you going to call it, Don's teatime?"

"In the Philippines the fourth meal of the day is known as the merienda. It's usually eaten between what we call lunch and dinner."

I couldn't tell if Don was serious, but considering the subject matter, I should have known he would have done his research.

"How would you know something like that?" I asked.

"Because I considered moving to the Philippines before I decided on Mozambique."

"Really? To the Philippines?"

He nodded. "Those were the two finalists. I was single and could move anywhere, so I wrote down everything that was important to me – and a country that eats four meals a day instead of three is always going to end up high on my list."

I watched Don closely to see if he was going to crack a smile or show any sign that he had been kidding. No sign of that.

"You guys are funny," Marsha smirked. "You'd actually move to the Philippines just because they eat four meals a day instead of three?"

"Obviously you've never seen this man eat," I said.

"That's true, but if I was going to live somewhere besides the United States, I'd move to one of the Caribbean Islands or Sweden. The relatives on my mother's side live in Malmo, and I always wanted to visit there."

"Isn't that directly across the bridge from Copenhagen?" Don asked.

"Have you been there?"

"No, but one of the Peace Corps workers I roomed with in Mozambique was from there. He said it was kind of cold."

"No colder than Minnesota," Marsha replied.

"That's true."

This was the first chance that I had to talk to Marsha about something besides Ray Gilbert. It was also the first time I noticed her smile. It lit up her face and highlighted her blue eyes. She was an attractive woman.

"What are your plans for today?" I asked her.

"I haven't made up my mind. I've been lucky to escape from Gilbert twice, but a third time might be too much to ask. How about you two? Are you still going to call him and pretend you're setting up a meeting?"

I told her about the call I had already made and the meeting at Trailhead Park.

"Good luck, but you should be careful. Ray Gilbert is nobody's fool and he won't be that easy to trick." She picked up the bill that the waitress left on our table. "How much do I owe?"

I grabbed the bill from her hand. "My treat."

***

"What do you think will happen at the park?" Don asked after we dropped Marsha off at her room.

"Not much, all we can do is watch and wait. Either Gilbert's men will show up or they won't."

"How did he sound when you talked to him?"

I shrugged my shoulders. "I'm not sure. At first it sounded as if he was surprised that I was calling, but I

166

think it's about 50-50 whether he bought my story and sends someone out."

"He might not have believed you, but I don't think he can take the chance."

TWENTY-ONE

TRAILHEAD PARK WAS located off Boulder Lane and Highway 620. We drove two blocks past the main parking lot, took a left onto Chestnut Ridge Road then another left onto Broken Brook curve. We ended up at the far north end of the park in a residential neighborhood. After parking the Tahoe in front of a vacant lot, I got out and examined the six-foot cedar privacy fence that obstructed our entry. I had to walk down about a block before finding a narrow opening between two of the fence posts. I motioned for Don to come over so he could take a look.

"We'll have to squeeze through those two posts, then climb up that hill. According to the map, we should have a clear view of the park and the surrounding area from there."

"Will you be able to make up that hill? It looks kind of steep," Don asked.

"I'll make it, just don't get in my way."

"If you get tired, let me know and I'll carry you the

rest of the way."

"Yeah, right."

Walking up an incline was easier with a cane than walking down one. It was more strenuous, but my equilibrium was better and I didn't worry as much about falling. On the way down, I had to be more conscious of taking a misstep and losing my balance.

I squeezed through the fence line first and Don followed. "You sure you're going to be okay?" he asked.

"I'll be fine."

"Okay then I'll see you at the top of the hill."

He jogged up the hill while I took my time. There were only two areas that gave me a problem, a large tree root that was difficult to step across, and an area that had eroded away and had loose gravel.

"Nice view up here," he said when I finally arrived.

From where I stood, I could see the parking lot, a covered patio with picnic tables, a set of swings and a playground. There was also a soccer field and basketball court. The only people at the park were a young girl throwing a ball for her dog, and a woman sitting at a picnic table with her two young children.

"We're an hour early, so let's get comfortable for the wait."

Don took the binoculars from their case and scanned the area. It wasn't long before I spotted a white minivan driving in our direction on Boulder Lane.

"Over there," I touched his shoulder and pointed. "Is that who I think it is?"

Don turned the binoculars and focused. "Two men in

the front seat." He continued to turn the focus dial. "Houston, I think we've identified our targets. Two men wearing sunglasses, over."

We watched the minivan drive past the park, do a U-turn a block down, and drive by again in the opposite direction.

"The cowboy must be on the disabled list," I observed.

We waited, but the minivan drove around the corner and out of sight. Five minutes later we noticed the same two men on foot.

I took the binoculars from Don. "They knew we'd recognize their car, so they parked it where they didn't think we could see it."

I watched them jog down the street trying to stay hidden behind the landscaping that grew between the sidewalk and the street. "It's the same two guys that abducted us." I took another look. "I'm satisfied that Gilbert is behind this."

"Just for the fun of it, let's sneak up behind them and give them some payback for tying us up yesterday."

I put the binoculars back in the bag. "They were just doing a job like we are. Who knows? Maybe we'll meet again and you'll get your chance."

I turned and started down the hill. Don sprang ahead, which was fine for me. It meant that I wouldn't have to keep up with him. He was waiting next to the car by the time I arrived. I handed him the keys.

"You drive, my legs are tired."

TWENTY-TWO

AFTER MULTIPLE SURGERIES for my gunshot wounds, I had been fitted with a fiberglass hip spica cast that covered my sternum from underneath both arms to just below my hips; it then continued down my right leg to above my ankle. While I wore the cast I was mostly bedridden. The only exercise I got was from a therapist who'd have me pull myself up by a metal bar attached to a set of weights that were anchored directly behind my head.

The fiberglass cast was a part of my life for a month, after which I was fitted with a smaller cast that allowed more movement. Gradually I was able to walk and use a real bathroom with a toilet and sink, instead of a bedpan and catheter - a welcome relief. When the smaller cast was finally removed, I felt like a wild animal must feel when freed from captivity.

For two months I learned to live with the restrictions of a cast during the day, but I never felt comfortable sleeping with it, unless I took a sleeping pill beforehand.

Even under the influence of a narcotic, I'd still wake up whenever I moved my torso. Sometimes my leg would spasm and I often experienced nightmares.

My mobility improved greatly after the cast was removed, but my sleeping habits haven't changed that much. I rarely slept longer than two hours at a time, and I became an early riser.

Don, on the other hand, was not.

He wouldn't wake up early unless there was a fire outside, and even then he'd want to know how serious it was before he decided if he was going to get out of bed.

***

It was another early morning start for me, so I decided to take a walk before it got too warm outside. But, when I was about to leave the hotel room, I noticed a card that someone had slid under the door. It was from Marsha and it was addressed to both of us:

Don and Tony,

I received some very distressing news last night. Greg Hoffman called to tell me that Randy Bealman's body was found floating on the Mississippi River under the Franklin Avenue Bridge in south Minneapolis. As can be expected, the information struck me hard even though I was sure it was coming.

I want to thank you both for your help, but it's time for me to leave Austin. Without the two of you I'm sure that Ray Gilbert would have arranged to have me killed also.

Thanks and I hope we'll see each other again some day!

Marsha

P.S. I left you a present, Tony. You're the detective, figure out what it means.

Hopefully it'll help you nail that bastard. Where I'm going I won't need it, but I will need truckloads of sunscreen!

Taped to the bottom of the card was a small bronze key, similar to the one I used to open my mailbox in the lobby of my apartment building. The letters AS-AUS 292 were printed on it. I brewed some coffee from the machine in the room, pushed the espresso button and walked over to Don's bed with a cup when it had finished.

"Wake up." I shook his shoulder.

"What, who did it?" he mumbled. He was still half asleep, so I gave him the coffee and waited for it to clear his head.

He finally sat up, put his feet on the floor and scratched his crotch.

"What time is it?"

"6:45 a.m."

"In the morning?"

"Yes, that's what a.m. means. Marsha took off and left us a note." I handed him the card and waited for him to read it.

"Do you think Gilbert was responsible?"

"I do now." I nodded. "Any idea what the letters on the key represent?"

"I can guess," he said as he inspected it. "Is there a train station or a Greyhound bus depot somewhere in this city?"

"Let me check." I looked around the room and found a visitor's guide on Austin that the hotel provided for its

173

guests. I started paging through it.

"There's an Amtrak station downtown at 4th and Lamar Boulevard, and a Greyhound bus depot at 914 East Koenig Lane."

Don pulled the key off the card and set it on the bed stand. "My guess is the key fits storage locker number 292 at the Austin Amtrak station."

"Why would she give us a key for a locker there?"

"It's obvious. After what happened to Randy Bealman, she's decided to leave town. Marsha's pretty savvy. Gilbert knows what kind of car she owns and instead of taking it across country where she could easily be followed, she went to the train station, bought a ticket and noticed the storage lockers. She'll probably sell her car for cash somewhere near the station, and head out of town by train. It's more difficult to track a train than an airplane flight."

The espresso had done its job; Don was now fully awake and obviously alert to the situation.

"How did you figure that out so quick?" I asked.

"That's what I'd do if I were in her situation."

"If you're right, I know what she left us." I ripped the page from the visitors guide and tucked it in my pocket. "Get dressed and I'll meet you in the car."

Twenty-Three

FROM OUR HOTEL, I followed the GPS instructions and drove south on Highway 183. I merged onto Mo-Pac highway and stayed in the right lane until I exited on 6th street. From there I drove west to Lamar Boulevard, then south to the Amtrak station. While I drove, I made sure we weren't being followed, then ate one of the four blueberry muffins Don had taken from the continental breakfast provided in the hotel lobby.

I parked in the drop off zone in front of the station and waited in the car while Don went inside. If he was right about Marsha buying a train ticket and selling her car, it meant that she'd soon be out of the reach of Ray Gilbert. I'm sure she'd admit that it was a mistake to have had a relationship with her boss, but that didn't mean she deserved the chain of events that had forced her to move, change her name and be on the run for the past year. We hadn't taken much time to talk, but from the little stretch we spent together, I sensed that she was intelligent and outgoing, and would probably be successful in whatever she decided to do. Maybe some

175

day I'd receive a card and she'd be living on a beach somewhere.

I hoped so.

While I waited for Don to return, I turned on my phone and checked my messages. Two calls had come in from Ray Gilbert, but he never left a message on either one. One of the calls came in after we had left the park yesterday. He would have figured out that I had lied when we last spoke on the phone. He must have also realized that I knew what Marsha really downloaded from his computer. If she disappeared, we'd be his new targets. How far he'd go to keep his secrets hidden was yet to be determined. Having Gilbert's hard drive in our possession might be a useful tool, but I still had to figure out the best way to use it.

It wasn't long before Don returned from the train station with a smile on his face and a paper bag in his hand. "Bingo!" he said, when he got into the car. "If I'm not mistaken we now have in our greasy little mitts a disk copy of Ray Gilbert's hard drive."

Our time in Austin was just about over. There was nothing left to accomplish. I didn't feel comfortable taking a plane back to Minneapolis, because it would have been easy for Gilbert to track our flight. Don called the rental car company and arranged for us to return the Tahoe to one of their lots in Minneapolis. He did have to give the rental car company his credit card number, but I didn't think Gilbert would be tracking him. We checked out of the hotel and headed north.

***

As far as 1100-mile road trips are concerned, the drive from Austin to Minneapolis was a simple one – we'd take the US Highway 35 north out of Austin for approximately 20 hours and we'd be home. We would set off that night at 9:30 p.m. and arrive at Don's apartment around 5:45 p.m. the next evening.

Besides a heavy downpour fifty miles north of Kansas City, the ride was an uneventful one. We stopped in Oklahoma at a truck stop to have breakfast, otherwise it was fast food, coffee and energy drinks from gas stations along the highway, with an occasional rest stop thrown in. The battery on my cell phone was nearly dead again and the charger was in one of my bags, so I used Don's phone to leave a message for Shelley and keep her up to date about our progress. I also wanted to make sure that she didn't say anything to Gilbert if he called.

While I drove, Don took a short nap, and I did the same when he was behind the wheel. The silence gave me time to think and prepare for how Ray Gilbert would react.

I was anxious to get home, so I drove the last six hours without a break. Once we arrived in Minneapolis, we picked up my car at my townhouse, dropped off the Tahoe at the rental car lot, and headed to Don's apartment where I dropped him off. We promised to talk in the morning.

That night I slept as well as I could have expected, considering my mind was still back on the highway, staring at the never-ending white line in the middle of the road.

I finally gave up and went to have breakfast at a nearby restaurant. All the food in my refrigerator was spoiled, and after the long drive from Austin with only junk food to eat, I was starving. After I finished eating I drove to Don's even though there would be a good chance that he'd still be asleep. I had forgotten to take my cell phone to alert him, so I was forced to wake him up the old fashion way.

"Were you really throwing rocks at my window?" Don asked when he finally opened the front door.

"It's what the situation demanded, your doorbell doesn't work."

"That was mature."

"Did you get any sleep?" I asked. Don was barefoot, wearing a sleeveless muscle shirt and plaid shorts. It was obvious that he had just dragged himself out of bed.

"That depends, what time is it?"

"You don't want to know," I said and walked past him.

He stood in the doorway and looked up at the sky. "Doesn't the sun usually rise about six in the morning this time of year?"

"How would you know that?" I asked as I sat down on his couch.

"I watched a program about it on the Discovery Channel. You're not planning on waking me up every morning at this godforsaken hour, are you?"

"I guess you didn't read the small type on the employment contract you signed."

"I must have been sleepwalking when I signed it,"

178

Don said. "I'm going to grind some coffee beans, would you like a fresh cup o' Joe?"

"You bet. Mind if I surf the Internet on your smartphone while I wait? I left mine at home."

"Here." Don handed me his phone and went into the kitchen.

With all the excitement in Austin, I'd been out of contact with the Internet for the last couple of days. I signed into my work email account and typed in my password. My inbox contained four new messages; all queries about my service. I replied by attaching our website URL and suggesting they call if they had a question.

I next typed in the web address for the Austin Statesman newspaper, as I wanted to read a columnist I had been following while I was there. There was a breaking news headline that I almost ignored, but something compelled me to read on. *The Austin police department is asking for the public's help in identifying a woman who was found dead...* I stopped reading and set the phone on the table. My hands were shaking and I couldn't think straight. It took a couple of minutes to calm down, before reading on:

The Austin police department is asking for the public's help in identifying a woman who was found dead of a gunshot wound on Monday morning. She was found in the back parking lot of the Amtrak train station on the corner of 5th and Lamar Boulevard, Austin. The woman was approximately 5 feet 7 inches tall, 125 pounds and had short blond hair. A police spokesman said the woman appeared to be about 30 years of age.

The woman who had been killed was Marsha. I was sure of it. I was now convinced that Ray Gilbert was responsible for the deaths of both Randy Bealman and Marsha Cummings. He was getting rid of anyone who had read the information from his computer and Don and I were the only people who were left.

"Don, get in here!"

He hurried into the living room balancing two cups of coffee. "What's up?"

"Read this." I turned his smart phone to landscape mode and handed it to him.

He stared at it then blurted, "Son of a bitch! Do you think it's her?"

There was more to the story and Don kept reading, but the sound of his voice was muted by the spinning sensation inside my head. Ray Gilbert's goons must have followed Marsha to the train station and killed her. I was sure of it, and I was partially to blame. He had used me to locate Marsha and I had led his men directly to her. I had also dragged my feet, when I should have listened to her.

Don was staring at his phone when I finally looked up. His fists were clenched and his knuckles were white. "She didn't deserve that." He set the phone down gently, as if he were somehow laying Marsha down to rest. He met my eyes. "How are we going to roll with this?"

"Right now all I can think about is driving over to Gilbert's office and grabbing that son of a bitch by the throat until his eyes pop out."

"I'm down with that."

I could see in the dark glare of Don's eyes that he meant what he had said. I took a couple of deep breaths and waited until I could speak. "Okay, let's think this through. We know what kind of man we're dealing with, and what he's capable of doing. Marsha is now out of the way, we know too much and it's only a matter of time before he comes after us."

"I get it, but do you have a plan?"

"Not yet, but I will. We need to stay in public areas, so he can't get at us."

"I agree," he nodded. "We're next."

"Big Fella, I'm sorry I got you into this mess."

"It's not your fault. There was no way that you could have known about Gilbert."

Don was right, but it didn't help the way I felt.

TWENTY-FOUR

I COULD NEVER hope to match Gilbert head to head in a battle. To be successful, I'd need the assistance of the public. The quickest way to do that was to go to the news media with the information I had. Discussing what I knew with my friends at the police force was out of the question because some of them might cover up the information if they were on Gilbert's payroll.

"How will we do that?" Don asked after I had explained my plan.

"By mailing information to the local television stations and newspapers. I'll include an introductory letter explaining how I came across the documents, and why I felt it was important. I'll also copy the donations he made from his private bank account to questionable organizations. I could even include Gilbert's email to the white supremacists, offering his allegiance. He never signed it but maybe there's a way the letter can be traced back to his computer."

I knew I was rambling, but I was frustrated.

Don wasn't convinced. "But they'll never take it

seriously. Ray Gilbert is the media's darling. You attack him without the goods to back it up, and you'll be the laughing stock of the city."

I didn't answer because I knew he was right. A lot of the information we had could be viewed as damning, but all Gilbert had to do was offer an explanation that people would believe. If it came down to a pissing contest between Gilbert and myself, it was no contest. He'd win the public vote.

"Maybe we can cast some doubt about his character," I offered.

"It would be more convincing if we could tie Gilbert to Marsha's murder. I still have the card she left in the hotel room - it's evidence that she believed he was out to kill her."

"But Gilbert didn't murder her directly, he only gave the order. He's too smart to be involved in a murder, and he could easily find a witness to say he was at the office at the time of the killing."

I sat back in the chair and finished my coffee.

"I'm going to head home and give a call to the Austin police department. I need to verify that it was Marsha who was killed."

"Okay, and I'll do what I was planning on doing this morning. I'm going back to sleep. Maybe when I wake up this will have all been a dream."

I drove home and used my home phone to call the tip line that was listed in the Austin newspaper. After a brief delay, I was connected to Officer John O'Reilly. At first he didn't want to answer my questions, and only wanted to know my interest in the deceased. I had to be careful because, besides Don's word, I couldn't prove I had an alibi as to where I was when the murder took place; although we had driven home from Austin and paid cash for the gas we purchased, I hadn't kept any of the receipts. I finally told O'Reilly about my previous duty as a police officer in Minneapolis, and my current job as a licensed private investigator. We exchanged names of people on the force that we both knew, and luckily for me, one of them was the current Police Commissioner in Austin who was hired as a former detective from Minneapolis. After that he lightened up.

"We believe her name was Marsha Cummings," said O'Reilly. "But she also had another woman's identification in her purse. Why were you looking for her?"

"We were hired by a former lover who wanted to get back together with her again. I would give you his name to verify that, but I signed a confidentiality agreement."

"That's fine for now, but depending on how our case progresses, I still might need that name."

"I understand. I guess we'll cross that bridge when we come to it."

He took my phone number and we promised to stay in touch.

I had been issued a gun permit at the same time as my private investigator's license, and I purchased a Kel-Tec PF9 pistol. It was sleeker and weighed less than the gun I had used as a police officer, which was a larger caliber and exposed to the public for a reason. The gun's power and size were meant to be a deterrent to the public. A private investigator's weapon needed to be hidden. The Kel-Tec was accurate up to fifteen feet, and that's the range I wanted it for. I kept the pistol under lock and key in a strong box in my bedroom closet.

I had only planned on carrying it in an emergency, but after what happened to Marsha, I decided to carry the gun until the situation with Ray Gilbert had been resolved.

TWENTY-FIVE

IF I WAS going to accuse the lieutenant governor of being a white supremacist, a believer in eugenics, and possibly a murderer, then I needed more evidence. I had to find something that proved beyond a reasonable doubt what Gilbert was planning to do, otherwise Don was right - any letter I sent to a reporter would be worth a chuckle and would soon find itself in the garbage bin.

I powered up my laptop and started with a search on white supremacy beliefs. I was aware of the principles of these groups, and from a personal point of view, I had worked with individuals who would be considered racists. We are a free country, and an individual has a right to his own beliefs, but when someone is in the position of authority like Ray Gilbert, then that individual needs to be scrutinized more closely.

I found several articles written about various groups in the US, including the National Socialist Movement, which was founded by George Lincoln Rockwell. The main difference between these groups and what Gilbert intended to do, was structure and money. The National Socialist Movement was disorganized and a majority of its members were just anti-government and anti-social fanatics. Rockwell himself was killed by one of the group's members.

Ray Gilbert was a leader, not a follower. I'm sure his plan was to cultivate his beliefs from the inside, as a member of government. As he pointed out in an email he had sent to one of his donors, he was fighting to take back America and allow the human race to move ahead as a species.

My research uncovered a definition for eugenics: *a social agenda to improve the genetic features of the human population by selective breeding and sterilization.* Interesting, I thought, it seemed to have parallels with Darwin's theory of evolution and the survival of the fittest.

In separate searches, I discovered information about the United States and its role with eugenics before WWII:

The concept of a white, blond-haired, blue-eyed master Nordic race didn't originate with Adolf Hitler. The idea was created in the United States and cultivated in California decades before Hitler came to power.

Eugenics was the racist pseudoscience that was determined to wipe away all human beings deemed "unfit" and preserve only those who conformed to a Nordic stereotype. Eugenics practitioners sterilized some 60,000 Americans before WWII, half of all procedures having been performed in California.

The practice of legal forced sterilization was an outgrowth of the eugenics movement – the idea that the genetic quality of

187

human populations should be improved by selective breeding practices, whereby society's elites would curtail unnecessary reproduction by the "feeble-minded."

The Rockefeller Foundation helped fund the German eugenics program that Josef Mengele worked in before he went to Auschwitz.

I was surprised to discover that even the United States Supreme Court had endorsed aspects of eugenics. In its infamous 1927 decision, the Supreme Court Justice, Oliver Wendell Holmes, wrote: *It is better for all the world, if instead of waiting to execute degenerate offspring for crime, or let them starve for their imbecility, society can prevent those who are manifestly unfit from continuing their kind. ... Three generations of imbeciles are enough.*

This was chilling reading that left me shaking and full of unease. It was a terrifying prospect that a future president of the United States could share these dangerous views.

I did a little further digging on Ray Gilbert, but the results were mostly positive news stories. The United States Congress only had an approval rating of 10%. That made me realize what a difficult task I was up against.

I turned off the computer, put a frozen dinner in the oven and turned on the television. While I waited, I stared at the screen, but it was only a diversion. The following morning I would contact the local media and prepare an informational letter about Ray Gilbert. I felt like David going up against Goliath, but it was the only viable option I had, based on what I knew.

I ate my high-fat, low-nutrition dinner, cleaned up

188

the kitchen and decided to get a little exercise. I usually tried to walk Max at least once a day, but I had not picked him up from Amanda's yet and I had been negligent in my own exercise. 9:30 p.m. was way too early for bed, and my brain was spinning with my plans for tomorrow, so I thought a walk would be the best option.

When I went to unlock my gun from the strong box in the bedroom closet, I noticed that something didn't seem right. The box was not against the wall like I had left it. I had purchased the strong box at the same time as the gun, so it was new, but I could see tiny scratches on the lock, as if someone had attempted to open it. I froze and tried to remain focused.

My four years in the military had taught me a soldier's discipline and how to focus attention on the slightest detail. I now saw that my clothes had been pushed to one side of the closet rod where I had hung them. I always made sure I left them hanging in the middle, because that is where they would have had to be in case of an inspection by the drill Sergeant. I backed away from the closet and inspected my bedroom. Someone had gone through my chest of drawers, pushing my socks and underwear to the side, and the drawers in my bathroom vanity were not completely closed.

I went back to my closet, opened the strong box, removed my gun and secured it in the holster on my belt. On my way out of the townhouse, I inspected the front door and noticed cuts around the wood next to the lock.

It had been forced open.

It was a professional job, something that the average homeowner would have overlooked, but I knew what to look for. Someone had broken into my house and searched it while I was gone. It wasn't difficult to know who was responsible, and what they were looking for. I grabbed my cane, took a light jacket and headed outside.

As I stepped outside, the cool breeze reminded me that I was no longer in Texas. I eased my way down the stairs to the street and decided to head toward France Avenue, which was usually crowded with shoppers.

I had only taken a couple of steps when I noticed a man gazing in my direction from across the street. He was talking on a cell phone while he leaned against the side of a building. I ignored his stare and continued my journey, but I couldn't rid myself of the feeling of being watched. I turned back to take a quick look; he was still observing me, making no attempt to hide it. I recalled what Marsha had said about seeing men outside her apartment. At the time I thought she was being paranoid, but now the same events were all hurtling towards me.

I had two choices, go back home and cut my walk short or head across the street and confront him. I wasn't big on running away, so I walked across the street and stood directly in his line of sight, about five feet away.

"Are you the guy who broke into my townhouse?" I asked.

He turned to the side and continued to talk on his phone as if I wasn't there. "Hey!" I shouted. "I'm talking to you!"

He continued to circle away from my line of sight, speaking into his phone.

"He just walked across the street and now he's standing next to me."

I followed in the same direction he was moving. "Next time you speak to Gilbert, tell him that he shouldn't send a boy to do a man's job. I'm not some helpless woman he can frighten easily. You got that?"

He still wouldn't make eye contact, so I walked closer and poked my index finger in his back. "Hello! Can you hear me?"

His eyes finally met mine. He took the phone away from his ear and placed it against his chest. "You want me to give a message to Ray Gilbert? Why don't you just tell him yourself?" He handed me the phone.

"Who is this?" I asked.

"Tony Crow..." I recognized Gilbert's voice immediately, although something had changed in his tone. His voice was deeper and more direct. He had only said a couple of words, but it was enough for me to recognize that the upbeat politician's voice of the past had disappeared. He spoke softly. "We have some unfinished business to take care of, don't we?"

"We sure do," I responded. "Let's meet somewhere, man to man, instead of having one of your men chase me around."

"You'll get your wish and soon. You can count on it." He hung up.

The man grabbed the phone out of my hand and walked away. I thought about following him to see where he was headed, but he was moving too quickly and I lost him in a crowd of people.

I no longer felt like taking a walk, so I went back to my apartment. It was time to finish my plan.

TWENTY-SIX

THE UPCOMING WEEKEND was my normal time to take Matthew. I'd been looking forward to seeing him and speaking with Amanda, but under the present circumstances, I didn't think it would be safe for me to do so. I used my freshly charged cell phone to give her a call and discuss my situation.

"Hey Tony, you back in town?" She sounded happy to hear from me.

"We got in late yesterday."

"Great, not that I want to get rid of him, but when are you coming over to get Max?"

"That's what I want to talk to you about. I know it's short notice, but something's come up and I don't think it would be a good idea for Matt to stay at my apartment this weekend. Once all the excitement cools down with what I'm working on, maybe I can take him another time, and make up for the lost weekend."

She didn't reply immediately, which I didn't take as a good sign.

"You don't think it's a good idea?" she repeated. "Of course Matthew won't mind, it'll mean he gets to keep Max a little longer, but I have to tell you that I'm disappointed."

"Believe me Amanda if there was anything I could do, I would. I'm sure if I explained the circumstances, you'd understand, but you're going to have to trust me for now."

Her voice grew scratchy. "Trust you? You must be suffering from amnesia. How many times have we had the same argument when we were married? How you'd call at the last minute to tell me you weren't coming home until late, and I'd discover that you were at a bar?"

"This is nothing like that."

"What a fool I am. How can I think about getting back together with you when it's starting all over again?"

"I'm sorry, Amanda, I really am." I didn't know what else to say. I could hear her breathing, but she didn't respond. "Amanda, are you still there?"

"Well, can you at least pick Matthew up at Howe school and drop him off at my house on Friday? I thought you were going to take him for the weekend, so I made a hair appointment at the time I usually pick him up. I can't cancel it now because the gal who cuts my hair has a three week waiting list."

"It's the least I can do. I'll pick him up at 3:30 p.m. and then wait at your house until you're home." She hung up and I felt like shit. I was deeply disappointed with her reaction, but I knew I had made the right decision. In time I was sure she'd understand.

***

After an uneasy night, I drove to work early the next morning and began to organize the letter I was going to send out to the news media. After giving it a lot of thought overnight, I decided to only include the information that would be the easiest to prove. Anything more than that, and I'd be leaving myself open to a lawsuit from Gilbert and his team of lawyers. On the other hand, a lawsuit was the least of my worries. I had to try everything that I could think of to stop a madman and murderer from becoming the next president of the United States.

I printed off copies of Gilbert's canceled checks that Marsha had copied from a list of deductions he had claimed on his taxes. I highlighted three donations that he made on a regular basis; he claimed the money went to scientific research, when in fact, the firm he was funding produced an infertility drug that was sold to third world countries as a polio vaccine.

I would also include the names of three Nazi members who were on the Gilbert Store's board of directors after WWII, and dates and copies of plane tickets he had purchased to speak at meetings across the country. The dates on the tickets and donations matched the dates of the meetings. Much of what I was sending was circumstantial evidence, and each individual incident he might be able to explain away, but when you added them all up, I felt his intentions were clear.

I heard Shelley arrive at 9:00 a.m. She peered inside the doorway to my office. "Hey boss, nice to see you again. How was the drive back?"

"Good, Shelley."

She came to my desk and handed me a stack of messages.

"A present for me?" I asked. "You shouldn't have."

"Consider it a welcome home gift. I've advised them that you were out of town and that you'd return their calls as soon as you were back."

"Any of them important? I'm going to be tied up with a project for awhile."

"No emergencies, but I've been thinking. Maybe some time when you're not busy, I could go with you and Don on an appointment. It wouldn't be too difficult for me to meet with these people when you're out of town. Otherwise they'll find another agency before you get back."

I paused for a moment. Shelley was smart and a quick learner. Besides working in the office and speaking to customers on the phone, it would be a benefit if she had hands-on experience with some of our clients. Down the road, she might even want to get her private investigators license.

"That's a good idea," I responded. "Let's talk about this more after everything calms down. Do you have a minute?"

"Sure, what's up?" She sat in a chair in front of my desk.

"I want to update you on what happened in Austin."

I told her about connecting with Marsha Cummings, how Don stopped her from being kidnapped, and how the three of us escaped from a warehouse in the country. Finally, I broke the sad news about the police finding Marsha's body behind the train station.

"That's terrible! Have they found her killer yet?"

"No, I don't think so. I also want to tell you that I appreciated the work you did while we were gone. It was asking a lot to leave you alone for almost a week."

"It got a little crazy a couple of times, otherwise I didn't mind."

We chatted for a little longer, and Shelley seemed pleased as she returned to her desk.

I removed the storage disk from my briefcase and connected it to my desktop computer with a USB cable. The documents and files were listed in folders on my screen under separate names. The entire disk was 500 Gigabits – that was too large to download to my computer, so I selected the same documents that Marsha had already pointed out. I highlighted all 136 of them and started to print them out.

While I waited, I checked online and located the address and phone numbers of the local newspapers and television stations. The Minneapolis Star & Tribune, and the St Paul Pioneer Press were in the Twin Cities area, along with four local affiliated television stations: KMSP, WCCO, KSTP and KARE. I called all six news departments and asked for the name of the head investigation reporter to whom I would address the envelopes.

Don showed up a little before 11:00 a.m. When he arrived, I called everyone together for a meeting in the conference room. I wanted to go over the information I was about to send out. If everything went as I hoped, the story might end up on at least one of the news outlets by the end of the week.

I began the meeting relating what happened outside my house the day before, then showed Don and Shelley the information I had printed off.

"Be prepared to hear from Gilbert or his lawyer," Don said. "Once the letters have been made public, I'm sure at least one of the reporters will call him for an interview to get a reaction."

"I've thought of that and maybe I should contact a lawyer myself. Besides suing me, any other ideas of what he'll do?"

"If I were him," Shelley ventured, "I'd try to discredit you. I'd explain to the reporters that you're angry because I fired you after you failed to produce the desired results in an investigation. I'd say that to get even, you've manufactured information to make a name for yourself."

"Gilbert's a politician," Don agreed. "He'll turn it around by saying he's standing up for the common man in the fight for the oppressed. You know, that kind of bullshit."

"Something tells me that's not the tactic he'll use," I said. "He doesn't have the personality to go on the defense. I think he'll attack, but I'm not sure how."

On my way home after work, I stopped off at my bank, rented a safe deposit box and placed the storage disk inside.

***

The letters went out in the mail late on Wednesday. With normal delivery, they'd be received on Friday or Saturday. My plan was to start making calls to the reporters on Monday morning, and I'd be able to gauge the level of interest and belief from the media. I was hesitant to include the circumstances surrounding Marsha's murder, but I decided to reveal that she was a former employee of the Gilbert Corporation, and that after she had provided us with information on Gilbert, she was found dead in the train station's parking lot. That would cause at least a few of the reporters to investigate, and my goal was to raise suspicions about Gilbert's private and political life.

Thursday passed quickly without much going on, which I took as a good sign. I was both nervous and excited to see the reaction my letters would receive. Friday arrived and I received my first call. It was a reporter from the Fox 9 television station. Shelley transferred the call to my office.

"Tony Crow," I answered.

"Mr. Crow, my name is Peter Elliot, I work for the Fox affiliate here locally. My station has asked me to give you a call after we received your rather interesting letter this morning. Do you have time to answer a couple of questions?"

"I have a few minutes, what would you like to know, Peter?"

"Well, to start with, could you give me a little personal history? I'm afraid I'm not familiar with the

Crow Investigation Service."

This was something I was prepared for, and was sure I'd have to repeat often. I started by explaining my military service, then my nine years on the Minneapolis Police force.

"And from what I understand, you were shot during an investigation. Is that correct?"

"That's correct." Good, Peter had done his homework before he called. That meant he was taking the letter I had sent seriously.

I talked about the incident when I was shot, the surgery I went through, the long recovery period and my decision to open my own private investigation service.

"And how did you meet Ray Gilbert?"

The interview lasted another 5 minutes. He asked most of the questions I thought he would, and there were no surprises. I couldn't tell if he believed me or not, but he finished the call by asking if I'd be available to do an interview on air. I said I was. "The sooner the better."

"Thank you for your time Mr. Crow. I, or someone from our station, will be in touch if we have any further questions."

Shelley entered my office as soon as I hung up. "How did it go?" I could tell she was excited.

"Good. He wanted my personal history and said he might be calling back."

"Well, if nothing else, maybe it'll be good for business."

I didn't correct Shelley because she had good intentions, but all I wanted to do was nail Ray Gilbert and make him pay for what he did to Marsha. I was growing in anger about the injustice.

Later, I answered a few calls about my service, and talked to a woman about her missing husband. After hearing my hourly fee, she decided to give him a couple more days to return. Apparently she was concerned about his whereabouts, but not $125-per-hour concerned.

I tried Amanda again to confirm that I'd pick up Matthew, but I also wanted to check and see if she was still angry. She didn't answer so I left a message. If she didn't return my call, I could talk to her this evening when I dropped off Matthew from school.

The rest of the afternoon flew by without any calls from the other news outlets. I had hoped for more, but maybe I shouldn't have. At the 5th Precinct an unsolicited letter could sit on someone's desk for weeks until the person in charge decided if it needed to be looked into. I'm sure it was the same way they ran the news. A television station must receive hundreds of unsolicited letters, and most of them are probably not taken seriously.

I was in my office talking with Don, when Shelley buzzed me on the intercom. "You told me to remind you to pick up your son."

"Thanks Shelley, I'll be leaving here shortly." I hung up and turned toward Don. "I'll get in touch if I receive any calls from a reporter, otherwise let's plan on talking sometime this weekend."

I said goodbye, took my briefcase and cane and headed to the car.

Howe Elementary is a PreK-5 school located in southeast Minneapolis. It wasn't a school that kids in Amanda's neighborhood would normally attend, but they had a special interest class that she wanted Matthew to take. She received the permission of the school board, but because there wasn't a school bus service available for that route, she had to agree to drive and pick him up each day from school.

On the way to my car, a couple of Jehovah's Witnesses approached and wanted to talk to me about joining their church. I was usually pretty good at avoiding those types, but this couple seemed to be a little more determined than usual. At one point they blocked my car door so I couldn't get in. To avoid a confrontation, I politely listened to what they had to say, accepted the literature they handed me, and got in my car and drove away. I didn't remember solicitors ever stopping me in a parking lot before, but maybe people were no longer answering their doors to religious callers.

I was about ten minutes late when I arrived at Matthew's school. Normally, he'd be waiting just inside the front door with a security guard, and he'd run out as soon as he saw my car. With the delay in getting stopped by the Jehovah's Witnesses, he must have gotten tired of waiting and went back inside. I parked my car close to the entrance and walked through the front door.

"Excuse me," I said to a woman who was passing by in the hallway, "I'm looking for my son. I was supposed to pick him up, but I'm a few minutes late. Is there somewhere he might be waiting?"

"There's not a designated room, but he could be in the principal's office. It's the third door on the left."

"Thank you, I know where that is."

I found Principal Linster's office, stepped inside and looked around. Matt was not in the room, but there was a receptionist who greeted me.

"I'm sorry to bother you. My name is Tony Crow and I'm here to pick up my son Matthew Crow."

"You're Tony Crow?" She looked confused. "A friend of yours has already picked up your son. You called me, don't you remember?"

"What?" I leaned on the desk with both hands. "I never called anyone at this school, now where's my son?"

"Mr. Crow, I'll need to see some identification please." While I searched my wallet, the receptionist was already on the phone. I didn't like what she had to say.

"Security, I need someone at Mr. Linster's office right away."

She took my license, held up the glasses that had been hanging around her neck and placed them over her eyes.

"Have a seat Mr. Crow." She handed back my license.

I couldn't believe what she was telling me. Apparently someone had called the school pretending to be me, claiming that I was running late because of a Jehovah's Witnesses conference, and therefore I was sending one of my friends to pick up Matt.

The receptionist was getting flustered. "You told me, or should I say, the man on the phone told me, that he didn't want Matthew to wait."

203

"Did you ask for identification from the man who picked him up?"

"There was no reason to, I already knew it wasn't you, and besides I thought Matt knew him."

"That's not possible," I said out of frustration.

Her head dropped and she exhaled slowly. "Nothing like this has ever happened before." With a nervous twitch she barely whispered, "I think maybe I should call the police."

While waiting for a detective to arrive, I tried to reach Amanda. The receptionist at the salon told me she was waiting for her hair to dry. I had to convince her that the call was an emergency and Amanda finally got on the phone.

"Tony what's going on?"

"I'm calling from Howe school. There's a problem."

"What is it? Is Matt okay?"

"When I came inside to see why he wasn't waiting for me, the receptionist said that someone else had already picked him up."

"What? Who? How is that possible?"

"We're still trying to figure that out, but I think you should be involved."

"I'll be there as soon as possible."

TWENTY-SEVEN

I WAITED OUTSIDE for the police to arrive, pacing the whole time. I knew Gilbert was responsible for kidnapping Matthew, but I didn't believe he planned to harm him. That wasn't his style. His goal was to intimidate me so I wouldn't talk to the news media. Harming Matthew would only strengthen my resolve to bring him down. At least that's what I hoped he was thinking.

I was not only concerned about Matthew, but also with how Amanda was going to react. Our only child was missing, and I knew she'd be just as angry and concerned as I was.

My hands were shaking, my throat was dry and I felt like having a drink, but to help calm my nerves, I did the best thing I could think of. I called Don and told him what had happened.

"We both know what this is about," he said. "Why don't we just cut out the middleman and I'll meet you at Gilbert's? Let's show that scum that he picked the wrong rattlesnakes to tread on."

Just then, a squad car pulled up and parked next to my car.

"The police are here, I've got to go. Call you later," I said and hung up.

I introduced myself to the officer as soon as he got out of his car. "My name's Tony Crow. It's my boy Matthew who's missing."

"I'm Officer John Barnes. Didn't you use to be a detective at the 5th Precinct Mr. Crow?"

"For nine years," I said and hurried with him to the principal's office.

"I've heard stories about your Dad."

Join the club, I thought.

When we arrived at the office, the receptionist was there with two other men. They introduced themselves as the principal, Les Linster and the school's security guard, Tom Victor.

I was in no mood for playing around. "Why is there a security guard at the school if not for this exact reason?"

Principal Linster glanced at the guard. "That's something we'll have to review later, but for right now, let's concentrate on finding your son."

I stared at him, prepared to argue forcefully, but decided he was right. The important thing was to locate Matthew. I recapped the events to the officer, while the other two men listened.

"And you have no idea who would claim to be you, then send someone else to pick up your child?" Officer Barnes asked.

"No one," I said. I didn't tell him about Ray Gilbert because I didn't think he'd believe me.

"Could this somehow be a friend's idea of a joke?"

"No chance."

He turned his questions to the receptionist, Debra McCarran. After she had explained how Matthew had come to be taken by a stranger, I filled out a police report with Amanda's and my contact information.

"I have to call this into headquarters," the officer said, "and give a heads up to the local FBI office. The Lindbergh law requires that I alert them when I begin investigating the kidnapping of a child under 12 years old. I'll be right back."

The officer left to use the police radio in his car. While he was gone, Amanda arrived, rushing through the front door toward the principal's office. Her hair was still wet and hadn't been combed, her eyes were red and she had a wild, frantic look about her.

"This is Matthew's mother, Amanda," I introduced her to the principal as she burst into his office.

"Tony!" She ran to me, and for a moment I thought she was going to give me a hug, but she stopped just short. "Have they found him yet?"

"No, they haven't."

I summarized events as best as I could, but it wasn't immediately sinking in. "I don't understand. Someone called the school and said they were you? Why would they say you were at a Jehovah's Witnesses conference?"

"I've been asking myself the same thing. I've already filled out a police report and given the officer a description of Matt. For now, all we can do is wait."

Amanda turned her anger toward the receptionist. "What right do you have to allow my son to leave this school with someone who wasn't authorized to pick him up?"

Officer Barnes returned from his squad car in time to calm Amanda. "I understand your anger, ma'am but let's concentrate on getting Matthew returned unharmed."

Amanda backed off; although she was visibly upset, she listened to what the detective had to say.

"Your son's description is being sent to every precinct in the Twin Cities area. The abduction is being broadcast as an amber alert on every highway sign in the upper Midwest. I've called the local FBI office, and you can expect a call from the agent who's been assigned to the case. That could be tonight or early tomorrow morning at the latest. We're doing everything we possibly can. Tony has given me both your cell phone numbers. We'll alert you as soon as we know anything."

"Amanda, come with me," I said. "The police know what they're doing."

We walked outside together and stopped next to Amanda's car. I felt anxiety, helplessness and anger all rolled into one. I was mad at the receptionist for not being more thorough, but I was also mad at myself for letting those so-called Jehovah's Witnesses delay me. There wasn't a word to properly express the way I felt about Ray Gilbert. But I knew it was important to stay calm, even though I had a massive knot in my stomach. I didn't want to upset Amanda more than she already was.

"I can stay over tonight," I offered, "if you need the company. It might be better for us both to have someone we can talk to."

"Tony, I have to ask you something." She avoided my comment. "Does Matthew's disappearance have anything to do with the case you're working on?"

I didn't know how to truthfully answer that question. "I'm not sure. I suppose it's possible."

"I just don't believe this!" she replied, glaring at me.

"Why don't I follow you home and we'll talk about it. I think it's important that neither of us are alone tonight." I couldn't let Amanda spend the night by herself. If Gilbert could take Matthew that easily, then he could also grab her.

"Why would someone take Matthew?" She burst into tears. "You're right. I'm a wreck and I need someone to talk to. I'll meet you at the house."

I drove behind Amanda, and once she had pulled her car into the garage, I parked in her driveway. She left the garage door open and I followed her inside. I was immediately greeted by a happy fox terrier.

"Hey, Max buddy, have you been a good boy?" I pretended to be excited but I wasn't in the mood for his happy greeting. He sensed my anxiety right away, turned around and lay down in his bed, never taking his eyes off of me.

Amanda walked around the house and turned the lights on. In the bright light it was even more apparent how concerned she was. Her unkempt hair was pointing in odd directions, and the skin around her eyes looked puffy and red.

"I'm going to make some coffee," she said. "Would you like some?" She tried to smile, but I could tell it was a struggle.

"Sure." I didn't think I'd be doing any sleeping that night.

Almost in a trance, Amanda went into the living room and set her purse on the table. Her face was colorless, and I could tell she was struggling to understand what had happened.

I heard her fill the coffee maker with water and go through the motions of setting cups and cream on a tray. It brought back memories of old times when we used to enjoy our morning coffee together before work, but I wished it could be under better circumstances.

I had only been inside our old house a handful of times since our divorce. Amanda had remodeled the kitchen with new appliances and cupboards, and the living room walls had recently been painted, but the oak buffet and bookcase we had bought on our first anniversary were still there. I recalled the way she had turned her head and smiled when the furniture was delivered.

Amanda returned from the kitchen, handed me a cup of coffee and sat down next to me. "You don't think anyone would hurt him do you?" she asked.

Would it do her any good to know that I thought it was Ray Gilbert behind Matt's abduction? It might be better for her to think that, instead of thinking he had possibly been taken by a pedophile. It was a difficult decision to make.

"No, I don't think so. I'm sure everything will work out and there'll be a logical explanation."

"How could there be a logical explanation, and why didn't you arrive on time to pick him up?"

"I was only ten minutes late and Howe school should have never let him leave with a stranger."

"I can't stand this!" She shook her head, put her hand to her forehead as if to stave off a migraine. She stared into her cup of coffee.

A photo album was on the table and I picked it up in an attempt to get Amanda's mind off things.

"I was showing that to Teri next door," she offered. "She comes over sometimes on weekends to talk and have coffee."

I opened it to the first page and realized that the album was filled with pictures of our son. Amanda moved her chair close enough for me to feel the warmth of her body. It felt comforting.

"I remember this one." I pointed to a picture of Amanda holding our newborn baby boy. "It's the first picture of Matt that I ever took. I think he was about twenty minutes old. I remember that he was no bigger than a loaf of bread."

Four more photos were on the next page. Each one brought up a different memory. "That's his one-year birthday cake," Amanda said. "You had to help him blow out the candle."

"And this one is his first Christmas. I'm sure you remember that we bought that tree from a vendor down by Lake Harriet, and we had to carry it all the way home. Do you recall the surprise we got the next morning?"

"You mean that bat? How could I forget? That thing still gives me the chills."

The tree apparently had been shipped from North Carolina with a hibernating bat on board. When the tree warmed up in the house, it woke the bat up. We found it hanging from the ceiling the next morning.

"As soon as you saw it hanging there, you ran to the bed and pulled the covers over your head. You wouldn't come out until I promised that it was gone."

Amanda laughed, and for a brief moment I think she forgot about Matthew, but the moment didn't last. I think we both felt a little guilty about laughing when our son was in the hands of a stranger.

I tried to keep her attention by looking at the rest of the album. There was a picture of Matthew holding his first baseball glove, and one from his first day in kindergarten, but looking at the pictures as a distraction didn't feel right. I closed the book and finished my coffee.

Amanda slid the album back into the bookcase. We had shared some brief memories, but now she couldn't even look at me. I was about to go to her when I felt my cell phone vibrate in my pocket. I thought I had turned it off. I pulled it out to read the text:

Look out the window asshole.

I looked at the sender.

Unknown.

When I heard a car door slam outside, it hit me. I rushed into the living room and looked out the window.

Matt was standing in the street by himself, while a black sedan sped away.

"Amanda!" I yelled and hurried outside. I wanted to get the car's license number, but I was so excited that I forgot my cane. I was only able to limp toward Matt. By that time the car had already turned the corner.

Matthew smiled when he saw me. "I thought you didn't want to take me this weekend," he said, and started to the house as if nothing had happened.

A moment later, Amanda rushed outside.

"Matthew!" She ran to him and gave him a hug.

"What happened to your hair?" he asked.

"Never mind about my hair, where have you been?"

"A friend of Dad's picked me up at school. Didn't he tell you?"

I grabbed Matthew by the shoulders and turned him so he was facing me. "Listen to me, son, where did *my friend* take you?"

"He drove me to his house and said you were going to come over later and pick me up."

"Where? Do you remember where you were?"

"No. He told me we were playing a game and he blindfolded me as soon as I got in his car. He didn't take it off until I was inside his house."

"What did he look like?"

"I don't know, did I do something wrong?"

"Matthew, I told you to never take a ride from a stranger." Amanda scolded. "We didn't know where you were."

"He said he was a friend of Dad's, so I thought it

213

would be okay if I went with him."

I touched Amanda's shoulder. "He looks fine. Yelling at him will only get him upset. Take him inside and I'll call the police and let them know that he's home. As long as he is safe, I'll spend the night at my place."

"Thank you, Tony." She grabbed Matthew's hand and made her way back to the house. I waited until they were inside and called Detective John Barnes.

"This is Tony Crow. My son was just brought back." I described the black sedan that had dropped him off in front of the house.

"He just showed up out of the blue?" he inquired.

"It looks that way, but I really haven't had a chance to talk with him yet. I wanted to call you first and thank you for your help."

"Did you get the car's license number?"

"No, I could only make out the color. I wasn't able to see the make, model or license plate."

"I'll call the FBI and tell them to call off the dogs."

I promised to contact the detective if Matthew had any knowledge of his abductors, then I hung up. I was about to put the phone in my pocket, when I received another text message.

Consider that a warning shot. Before you pull another stunt like you did with that reporter, remember we know where your wife and son live. If anything like this happens again, expect to see them disappear, and next time it'll be for good. Sweet dreams chump!"

I looked both ways down the street to see if anyone was around, then got into my car and took a deep breath.

Peter Elliot must have called Ray Gilbert to get his reaction, like Don thought he would. I was stupid for not being prepared, and almost paid a heavy price. I also needed to speak with Matt again to see if there was anything he could tell me about the man who picked him up.

I gave Don a call and filled him in with the details. "Matt is safe at home with Amanda."

"That's great. What happened?"

I brought him up to speed, including the text messages and the warning.

"You know this is not the end of it, don't you?" he warned.

"I know, and I need to ask a favor."

"Shoot."

"Gilbert already showed me how easy it was for him to take Matt. He could come back and…"

"You want me to watch Amanda's house tonight? I think I might still have an unused plastic container around here somewhere."

"Thanks, I'll only need you for half the night. You usually don't get to bed until late, and I'm an early riser, so if you could take the first shift, I can go home and take a quick nap. I'll relieve you about 2:00 a.m. I'd rather not tell Amanda because it will only worry her."

"I'll park down the block - she won't know I'm there."

I gave him the address and told him that I'd wait until he arrived.

TWENTY-EIGHT

AFTER DON SHOWED up I returned home and called Amanda. I wanted to make sure they were both all right. Matt answered the phone and was his normal chatty self, which was a good sign. It didn't sound like he even knew why we were upset.

Amanda was holding it together, and didn't bring up the question that went unanswered about the reason for Matthew's disappearance.

Even more than usual, I had a difficult time getting to sleep that night. The coffee didn't help, but it was more to do with Ray Gilbert attacking my family, and how powerless I felt to stop it. My going to the media must have really struck a nerve, delivering a potentially lethal blow to his election campaign.

I stared at the ceiling until my alarm went off at 1:00 a.m. I got out of bed and went through my normal morning routine. I took a shower, got dressed and drove to Amanda's house. I found Don sitting in his van at the end of the block with a pair of binoculars in one hand, headphones over his ears, and the other hand was keeping beat on the steering wheel to a song he was listening to.

"Hey boss," he greeted me when I knocked on the side window of his car.

"Everything's quiet. She only went to sleep about an hour ago – that's when all the lights went out. Did you want me to do this again tonight? I don't have a problem staying all night, if you need your beauty sleep."

"Thanks, but let's see how it goes tonight. I might just hire a security guard for a night or two. There's a good chance I'm going to need you wide awake during the day."

I parked my car a little farther down the block and made myself comfortable, but not too comfortable. Overnight surveillance was a chore that I had gotten used to during my first two years on the force. More often than not, we'd be watching a suspected drug dealer's house, after neighbor complaints of unusually high traffic in the area.

I brought a paperback book I had recently purchased, and the time went by relatively quickly. The lights on Amanda's house came on again about 6:30 a.m., and I took that as a sign that she was fine.

I drove home, changed and headed into work. Even though it was Saturday, I requested that Don meet me at the office. On my way, I stopped at A Baker's Wife and picked up a sack of pastries. It was a poor excuse for breakfast, but I didn't feel like stopping anywhere on the way to get something more substantial.

I came into the office after 8:00 a.m. and was surprised to see that Shelley and Don were already waiting. I handed the bag to Don because I was confident he knew what to do with the contents.

Don looked me over with concern and spoke with an early morning croak. "I took the liberty to call Shelley in for an emergency meeting. I knew you'd want to meet and discuss what happened yesterday."

"I didn't think I'd see you until at least noon."

"This is more important than sleep."

"Thank you, I appreciate that," I said. "Let's meet in the conference room. First, I need a coffee. Anyone else want anything?"

"We've had our coffee while we were waiting."

I poured out the almost empty pot, filled it with water, packed the fresh ground beans into its receptacle, and turned it on. I stared at the bubbling pot as I thought about what I wanted to say. Once it had finished, I filled my cup, grabbed a few napkins and headed to the conference room. Don and Shelley were sitting at the conference table with a mixture of donuts, croissants and kolaches on a paper plate.

"Shelley, you're free to offer your thoughts and opinions, but I want you to take notes of the meeting, please."

She lifted up her legal pad to show me she was prepared. I started the discussion. "Let's talk about our options."

"First," Don began, "it might be a good idea to understand why Ray Gilbert picked you to locate

218

Marsha."

"There were a couple of reasons. I had just started a new company with only three employees and if we discovered any information that made him look bad, we wouldn't be as convincing as one of the larger agencies if they wanted to discredit us."

"Okay, what else?"

"With my police background, I had the means to locate her and if Gilbert's plan was to kill Marsha Cummings all along, he would only have to get rid of two more witnesses"

"You think he meant to kill all three of us?" Don questioned.

I nodded. "At Trailhead Park he did and so far he's only accomplished a third of his goal." I looked at Shelley. "Unfortunately you might also be added to that list."

"It's something I'm going to have to deal with," she conceded.

"So what do we do now?" Don asked.

"When he kidnapped my son, it was Gilbert's way of sending me a message that I should immediately forget about contacting reporters. What he wouldn't expect is for me to up the ante by going on the offensive."

"How would you do that?"

"That's the million dollar question." I found myself nervously tapping my fingers on the table. "I just don't understand how he knew, where and when I was going to pick up Matt. I'll check my car for a GPS device, but that wouldn't explain how he knew where I was going before I arrived. He even sent a couple of phony Jehovah's Witnesses to delay my departure." I paused. "Maybe I should pay a visit to an old police buddy of mine."

"It's worth a try," Don said.

"For now it's important that we stay safe – that means not going anywhere alone, especially after dark. I know that's a difficult thing to ask, but it's better than the alternative."

TWENTY-NINE

LIEUTENANT PAT WILLIAMS was the head of the Technical Surveillance Unit at the 5th Precinct when I was an officer. We had worked closely on a couple of projects in the past, and about five years ago he was credited with the development of the DeltaRay, a fake cell phone tower that the Minneapolis police used to track cell phone signals inside vehicles, homes and insulated buildings.

The tower could be placed near a suspect's residence and it would intercept cell phone calls before they were relayed. The DeltaRay was considered to be a major national achievement, and it led to Pat being given an award.

He was a good guy, and if there was such a thing, I thought of him as some kind of police nerd, a misplaced hippie. He even wore his hair a little longer than was recommended in the police handbook, but no one questioned it because he rarely dealt with the public.

It had been a while since we last spoke, and I hoped

he might be able to help me with my problem. I also wanted to get an update on any new surveillance devices that he knew about.

As soon as our meeting was over, I called Pat from my desk. I had expected to leave a message on his answer service, and was surprised when he picked up the phone on a Saturday.

"Tony Crow, long time, no see. How have you been, buddy?"

"Good, Pat, and you?"

He brought me up to date with his wife, Barbara, and their three children. The youngest son, Jacob was in the sixth grade at the same school Matthew attended. I followed with a rundown on my business.

"Is there a time that I can drop by and talk to you about one of my cases? I've got a problem, and I want to speak with an expert. It's important."

"Well, the expert is on vacation, but I'm available," he laughed. "If you're not busy right now, how about lunch in my office?"

"I'm surprised that you have to work today."

"Since the budget cuts by our lawmakers, six days a week is the new norm. I wonder how much money they actually save with a hiring freeze, when they end up paying the overtime to the people who are forced to cover the extra day."

"I gave up trying to understand politicians a long time ago."

"On your way over could you stop at Mike's Bar and pick up a Juicy Lucy with fried onions? You might not

222

like my breath, but you'll have my undivided attention for an hour. How's that for a trade off?"

"If I remember correctly, onions might actually be an improvement."

"That was uncalled for," he chuckled.

"I'll see you about 1:00 p.m."

The 5th Precinct station was located at the intersection of West 31st and Nicollet Avenue in south Minneapolis. I stopped at Mike's Bar and got Pat's order before driving to my old station.

Pat Williams's office was in the back of the building, next to the technical surveillance lab, and I had to walk through the main lobby to get there. This would be my first time back to the same building where I had worked for nine years before my injury. As soon as I walked in, I could smell the familiar aroma of stale perspiration and cheap cologne. The building was old and needed renovation; it had suffered from years of people passing through at all levels of hygiene. I had to wait because the officer at the front desk was busy, but then I heard a friendly voice behind the counter.

"Hey, Crow!" It was Sergeant O'Hara. "How they hangin'?"

The officer behind the counter who had been speaking to a woman, frowned at what the sergeant had said, but it didn't bother either of us.

"Just like you left them Sarge, swingin' free and easy."

"Free and easy? What a coincidence. That was my first wife's nickname, if I remember correctly."

223

He laughed and came from the back of the counter and slapped me on the back. "What brings you to our neck of the woods?"

"I have an appointment with Pat."

"I should have known you were here to see Williams by the grease spot on the bag you're holding. Is this about a new case, or did you get a job making deliveries for the bar down the street?"

"Who knows? If you don't refer some business my way, I might end up as a delivery boy. By the way, I want to thank you for the referral you sent me last month, Ray Gilbert. What do you know about him?"

"Ray Gilbert, the lieutenant governor? I never sent him to you. I've never even met the man. You must have me confused with someone else."

"Are you sure?"

"Positive. I think I'd remember if I talked to the lieutenant governor. Anyway, it's nice to see you again, but some of us around here have to work," he said with a smile. "Just go on back, he's expecting you."

I was sure that Greta Bergren had said they received my name from Sergeant O'Hara at the 5th Precinct, and when I brought it up with Ray Gilbert at his house, he didn't deny it.

I passed down a familiar hallway with its black and white scuffed tile floor, and a false ceiling with fluorescent lights. I had gone down the same hallway many times, but always as a part of the police force. The surveillance cameras hanging from the ceiling felt different now that I was a member of the public.

Pat was talking on the phone when I entered his office. His feet were on his cluttered desk, which included a half-eaten apple and an overflowing ashtray. I handed him the bag with the burger in it.

He smiled, placed the palm of his hand over the phone and whispered. "You remembered, excellent. There's cola and bottled water in the refrigerator if you want anything to drink. Grab me a cola while you're there. I'll be with you in a second."

I retrieved Pat's drink and waited for him to finish his call.

"Tony!" He stood up and we shook hands.

"What's with the ashtray?" I asked after we sat down. "Smoking has been banned in public buildings for quite a while."

"What are you going to do, call a cop?" He grinned.

"I would but there's never one around when you need them."

Without mentioning any names, I told him about a client I was working for, and a problem I was having with surveillance. "While I was in Austin, someone appeared while I was doing an investigation, and now in Minneapolis it's happened again."

"Give me the details," Pat said.

I started by describing the two stakeouts.

"Did you check your car for a bug?"

"Thoroughly, and I also inspected the hotel room I was staying at."

"I know your record as a police officer, so I'll take it for granted that you know what you're doing. How
225

about your cell phone, is it clean?"

I shrugged my shoulders. "I think so, I know there aren't any apps on it that I didn't install."

"How do you know that?"

"Because I can see the icons of the apps on the screen." I pulled the phone out of my pocket and powered it up to show Pat what I had. "I know I've installed all of these."

I waited while he finished eating his burger. He wiped his face and hands with a napkin, and threw the bag into the trash.

"Even though it's only been a year since you were a cop, technology has changed. Let me see that."

I handed him my phone.

"Not being able to see an app on your screen doesn't mean there isn't one installed."

He stood up, walked over to a wall cabinet and pulled out two adapters that were inside a drawer.

"What are you going to do with that?"

"Test your phone's power supply. I can already feel that it's running hot, although there could be a number of reasons for that. I noticed you had to turn the power on before you could show me your screen. Why did you do that?"

"The phone is getting old, and it's been losing power quickly."

He nodded. "And how about the screen, does it seem to be flickering more recently?"

"Yes, now that you mention it, but I thought that had to do with not getting a clear Internet connection."

He moved over to his computer. "I have a program on my computer to test for spyware. Hold on a second, and let me see if this thing works."

He stuck the smaller adapter into the power supply and the other plug through the headphone jack. After a short delay, a list of the apps that were installed on my phone appeared on his screen. "Come over here and take a look at this."

I walked over to where he was standing.

"Do you recognize all these apps?"

I read them to myself: YouTube, the Weather Channel, address book, mp3 player, photos and Skype. "Wait a minute, what's this?" I pointed to one of the icons. "HiSpy? I never downloaded that one."

"And that's the one I was worried about. HiSpy enables the installer to listen to your phone calls and monitor your GPS. The 5th Precinct has an account on the developer's website, and just about all our detectives use it, or another app similar to it."

"How does it work?"

"If someone installs the app on your cell phone, all they have to do is add your phone number to their account, and every time you make or receive a call, an email alert is sent to the installer, and they can go to their computer and listen or record the conversation. It also allows them to track your location through the GPS device on your phone or they can receive a copy of all the text messages and emails you send. Give me your phone number and I'll show you how it works."

I gave Pat the number and after he signed into his

account, he typed it in.

"Come over here and look at this."

My name and location appeared on a map of Minneapolis. According to the map, I was on the corner of 31st & Nicollet Avenue. I did a double take and looked at the screen on my phone. "It doesn't show anything on here," I observed.

"That's because it's totally invisible to you. They market the product to parents who want to keep track of their kids. There's a warning on the company's web page that states you have to inform the person whose phone you're installing the software on, but of course, no one does that. What kid would use a smartphone when their parents are aware of every place they go, what they're saying and every text message they send."

"That's unbelievable."

Pat frowned. "There's more."

"How's that?"

"The person who's installed the app is also able to listen to your phone's surroundings, even if you're not using it."

"My surroundings? What does that mean?"

"To use that part of the software is a little more tricky, and it's the reason your phone has been losing power so quickly. Let me show you."

He typed the phone number in again at a different location on the same site then checked a box at the bottom of the page. "We need to wait just a minute, now say something."

"Like what?" I asked.

After a short delay, I heard my voice on his computer say *like what?* then *like what?* again.

"The second time is the echo of the phone hearing it on the computer. Let me turn this thing off."

Pat closed his web browser.

"Will it work even if the phone's in my pocket?"

"In your pocket, a desk drawer, anywhere. The only requirement is that the phone's power is on."

"You're kidding!"

"A little scary isn't it? The only negative about it is that it drains the battery on your phone quickly, so they can only leave it on for short periods of time before the phone begins to heat up."

I shook my head in disbelief. "Can you tell if someone is listening in now?"

Pat held my phone in the palm of his hand. "I'll give it a minute to cool down.

Nope, not warm enough." He set my phone on the desk. "Have you given your phone to anyone recently?"

"No, I make a point to never..." Then I remembered Ray Gilbert asked to use my phone when I was at his house. He even went away from my view for several minutes while he was supposedly using it. More than enough time to install the software.

"That son of a bitch!"

"I take it that's a yes. Do you want me to remove it? All I'd have to do is highlight the icon on my screen and delete on my keyboard."

"Hold on, let me think about that."

229

At the time it wasn't clear how, but it was possible that I could turn this to my advantage. I'd have to get another phone to use for a while, but that shouldn't be a problem. "Can I bring it back and have you delete it later?"

"Any time, but it might cost you another trip to Mike's."

"That's doable."

Pat unhooked my phone from his computer and gave it back to me.

"Make sure you keep the power off," he instructed, doing his best Rod Serling imitation. "Otherwise someone might be listening."

"Good point." I immediately shut down the phone and put it in my pocket.

Pat explained how the technology would soon be moving to the skies "You ain't seen nothing yet," he said.

"Are you referring to drones? I've heard about those things."

Pat nodded. "As soon as that happens we'll have access to every cell phone conversation, every piece of GPS data, all media interactions and every credit card transaction of anyone who owns a cell phone within reach of a drone. After that, all we'll have to do is secure a warrant."

"It looks like it's time to start using my landline more often."

We spent the rest of his lunch break discussing my business, and how it was doing. At 1:00 p.m., he told me that he had to get back to work. "Thanks a lot Pat. I'll call you either way if I want that app removed."

"Like the Eagles once sang, *Take it easy.*"

***

When I left Pat's office my head was spinning. It was obvious that if you wanted to stay connected to the Internet, use a GPS device or cell phone, then complete privacy was no longer possible - and I'm not referring to invasion by just private citizens. The federal government, no matter what they say, is also listening to our cell phone conversations, and reading our emails.

Some people argue that if you haven't done anything wrong, then you have nothing to worry about, but I wonder if they'll feel the same way when a police officer or government agent arrives at their door without a warrant, and wants to search their home.

I can almost see it now: the government will have the slogan *If you haven't done anything wrong, then you have nothing to worry about* painted on the side of police vehicles. Our constitution was designed to protect our freedoms by imposing laws on those who hold political power, not the other way around.

Changes in technology were progressing a little too fast for my comfort.

THIRTY

I GAVE DON a call when I returned home so I could use my home phone. I wanted to update him about my conversation with Pat Williams.

"So," Don sighed into the phone. "Gilbert knew where we were going by listening to your cell phone conversations."

"He apparently installed the software on my phone when I was at his house. After that, he received a copy of every text, email and phone conversation I had, which included the GPS coordinates of our locations. That's how he found out we were at Marsha's house, at the credit union in Burnet, and where and when I was supposed to pick up Matt."

"He could listen to your phone calls?"

"Probably not live, but he had access to each conversation I had as an MP3 file on his website."

"Wow! And the guy who told you that was someone you used to work with?"

"Pat Williams. We worked together at the 5th

Precinct. His specialty is technology and surveillance, but our paths would cross every once in a while because we worked in the same building."

"Okay, so what's next?"

"The first thing I'm going to do is quit using my cell phone, but besides that I've received two more calls from reporters about the information I sent out. One of them has requested that I do an interview on a newscast."

"I think that's the way to go."

"It's beginning to look like it's my only choice. Once the story has broken, reporters will be able to dig up a lot more dirt than I can. I just have to make the information sound credible so they'll believe it."

"Gilbert and his team of lawyers might be able to convince people otherwise, but I don't think he'd dare do anything to you or your family after it's been made public. It would be too obvious who was responsible."

"By the way, I'm going to purchase a new cell phone. I'll call you with the new number in the next day or two. Until then make sure you don't call the old number. I'm not going to turn it on unless I can figure out a way to use it to my advantage."

"Why not just delete the software and be done with it?"

"Pat said he could do it any time, but I might find a use for it."

"Until then, it's active on Pat's computer. If his department has an account for the same software, aren't you afraid they could use it to follow you around?"

"No, he's got more important things to do than that.

At least I hope he does, but just to be safe, I'll make sure I charge up the battery first and then shut it off."

That afternoon I called Phillip Donnelly, the owner of Donnelly's Security, to arrange for protection for Amanda. I knew him from my first year on the police force before he retired to start the security company. I was confidant that he'd watch the house and take the appropriate steps if he saw anything suspicious.

I gave him my billing address, my home and work numbers, and he promised to keep me updated on a daily basis.

Some security services were used more for peace of mind than actual results. I was once told that a sign from a security service on the front door or in the yard of your house was almost as effective against a common burglary as having the house wired. But when you're up against professionals like Gilbert's men, that wouldn't be effective.

That evening I was preoccupied with whether to give an interview or not. Don was right, Gilbert might end up suing me, but once the accusations were made public, he wouldn't hurt Matthew or Amanda. Their wellbeing was my main priority.

I went over in my mind what kinds of questions a reporter might ask and how I'd answer them. I didn't want to sound as if I had an agenda, only that I was concerned about the motives of an elected official.

***

Monday morning when I got to work I received a call from Peter Elliot at Fox9 news. I asked him if he was going to also contact Ray Gilbert.

"In a significant story like this, we must contact both sides and give the accused a chance to respond. When that will take place is out of my hands."

We talked at great length about what the interview would cover, and we agreed that I'd do it at his station on Thursday afternoon. The interview would be taped, and if the manager of the station believed it was worth airing, it would be shown on the 6:00 p.m. telecast that night. When I hung up, I was convinced I was doing the right thing.

While at home on Tuesday morning, I received an all-clear message from Phillip Donnelly. It was the second time he had called after having one of his guards watch Amanda's house. That eased my mind.

THIRTY-ONE

AS SOON AS I entered the office on Wednesday afternoon, Shelley handed me a message. It was from a gentleman named Bill Everett. He had informed Shelley that he was a business owner in Minneapolis, and he wanted to merge his company with one of his competitors. It was to be a joint venture and Bill wanted to hire a third party to conduct a background check on his potential partner.

I gave him a call.

"What kind of business is it?" I asked, after we had introduced ourselves.

"A fitness gym. Our two companies cater to a similar clientele, and a merger would allow us to compete against some of the larger national chains."

"Why would you want to do a background check on the other owner?"

"I'm familiar with him through business dealings we've had in the past, but I'm not sure what his personal credit rating is. If we're going to be partners that could affect me somewhere down the line. All I'm asking is that you conduct an investigation, ask around and find out what kind of guy he is - then write a report about what you've discovered. It's pretty straight forward."

"How did you get my name?"

"My receptionist did a Google search and found your website. It sounded like what I wanted, so I called the Better Business Bureau and you checked out."

"By the way, what's the new business going to be called?"

"Fitness on the Go."

I was hesitant to sign a new client with everything else that was going on, but with the Gilbert dealings occupying most of my time for the past month, I thought I could use the diversion. More importantly, I needed the money. Because of the recent developments in the case, I knew it would be a waste of time trying to bill Gilbert for the extra time I had spent.

I agreed to meet with Bill Everett at his office in Minneapolis at 8:00 p.m. that night. The address I was given to check out was 718 Glenwood Avenue North. According to the GPS in my car, that would place their office in north Minneapolis near the Theodore Wirth golf course. I drove by the building to see if I could see the name of the company on a sign, but the building wasn't well lit and I couldn't make out the directory. There was no on-street parking available so I parked in a vacant lot a block away and walked back.

The street was deserted and dimly lit. It was a cool clear night and I pulled my sweater up to cover my neck.

In the distance I could see the IDS tower and the Wells Fargo building in downtown Minneapolis. I kept going until I came to a restored brownstone building with 718 over the entryway. There were five steps that led to the entrance and no handrail, so I carefully walked up the stairs and stopped at the directory. I searched for Fitness on the Go, but suddenly, something didn't feel right. As far as I could tell, the building didn't appear to contain commercial units, and I could see from looking through a plate of glass on the front door, there were no lights on inside.

I took a step back to get a better view and heard footsteps behind me. Before I could turn around I felt a sharp pain on the back of my head, saw a quick flash of light and everything went black.

THIRTY-TWO

A PULSATING PAIN felt as if a sledgehammer was driving a steel spike through my brain. I thought I'd had too much to drink and must have overslept, but when I tried to move my hands, it felt like I was underwater and everything was moving in slow motion.

A dense fog filled my head and refused to clear. In the distance I could hear the mumbled sound of a voice, and then another, but neither of them sounded familiar.

"Hey, wake up," A man pushed my shoulder. "I can see your chest moving so I know I didn't kill you," he laughed.

He pushed me again, a little harder this time. "Come on man, I didn't hit you that hard. Open your eyes."

My brain-fog cleared a little, but I was still in intense pain. Slowly I forced my eyelids to open.

"Good, you're awake. Long time, no see," he chided. "I was a little worried about you for a while. I thought I might have used a little too much force as payback for your guy hitting my partner over the head and locking him in the closet."

Even though I was having difficulty focusing, I knew the man standing in front of me was the guy in the sunglasses, and one of the two men along was the cowboy who had abducted us and brought us to the warehouse. I reached down to find my pistol with my left hand, but it was gone.

"Looking for this?" He showed me my gun and slid it under his belt behind his back.

"That wasn't very nice of you to trick us back at that park in Austin."

"What happened?" I mumbled, but I already knew the answer. I'd been lured on a bogus appointment and hit over the head.

"Before we go any further, how about we make an agreement and I won't have to do this again."

He flicked the side of my head with his index finger, but it felt more like I'd been struck by lightening. I held my breath and waited for the pain to lessen.

"Okay, just so we understand each other. I'll ask the questions. Nod your head if you agree."

I tried to nod, but it was more of a tic.

"Good. Let's begin this session with a reward. You've been out for a while and my guess is that you'd like a glass of water."

"Yes," I gasped.

"Drink it slowly." A cold glass was placed in my left hand. My right hand was tied to the arm of the chair. The water tasted refreshing and cooled my parched throat.

"We're making progress. Now the first question is an

important one. Does anyone know you're here?"

"Where am I?"

"Okay, stupid question. Let me rephrase it. Does anyone know where you were going tonight?"

I was slowly regaining my senses, but it was a struggle. Shelley had answered the original call from the man who said he wanted to hire me, but besides a phone number and a name, I didn't know if she wrote anything else down.

"Time's up. Do you want me to slap your head? Believe me I can do it a lot harder than the last time."

"No, no I'll answer. It's possible that my secretary might know."

"What does that mean, it's possible that she might know?"

"I wrote it down in my calendar that she has access to."

"Your appointment was for 8:00 p.m. Isn't that a little late for a receptionist to still be working?"

I nodded and regretted it. Even the slightest movement of my head was painful.

"Okay, now the questions begin to get more important. You know why we've brought you here, don't you?"

"Gilbert," I whispered.

He bent over and spoke into my ear. "That's right, Ray Gilbert."

My eyes were still not focusing, and I could tell that both of my legs were tied to the chair. Only my left hand was free.

241

"Mr. Gilbert is a reasonable man. The only reason he let your son go was that he believed you'd understand that it was only a warning, and you'd quit this nonsense. Now we've been told by a reporter that you're talking about all the lies that whore bitch tried to spread about him."

"What do you want?" I flinched when he brought his hand to the side of my face. He stopped just short.

"Didn't I already explain it to you? I ask the questions."

He got up and walked over to his partner. They talked quietly before he returned. "I want to know what you believe you have, and what you are telling the reporter."

I had to quickly decide the best way to handle the situation, and with a piercing headache, that wasn't going to be easy. I knew if they wanted me dead, I'd already be pushing up daisies, so I had something they believed was important. "I have the information that Marsha Cummings copied from Gilbert's computer."

He waved his hand as if he didn't care. "That's old news, and we're already aware of that. What we want to know is where you're keeping it? We've searched your car, so we know it's not there."

"It's in a secure place, but I'll only give it to Ray Gilbert."

"That's funny. You're tied up with two armed men who've been instructed to not let you go under any circumstance, and you're making demands?"

He was right. I wasn't in the best situation, but I had

242

to bluff my way through until I could think of a better idea. "Ray Gilbert is the man who hired me, and he's the only person that I'll negotiate with. How do I even know you work for him?"

"Who else do you think I work for, a competing television station?" He laughed then narrowed his eyes. "You, my friend, have some nerve."

This time he slapped the side of my head with an open hand and didn't hold back. My eyes fogged up and I had to grit my teeth to show him that I wasn't hurt – but if I got out of this situation alive, he was going to pay.

"Okay, now I'll give you another reward. Do you see how this works? You get to ask me a question."

"What time is it, and how long have I been out?"

He looked at his watch. "It's 10:45 p.m., and you've been in dreamland for about three hours."

"Where did you take me?"

"You're pressing your luck." He turned to his partner and nodded. "That's enough for tonight. If he pisses on the floor, I don't want to be the one who has to clean it up. Drag him to the bathroom, untie his legs and allow him to use the john. After he's finished, tie him up again and we'll deal with him in the morning. I need to talk to the boss and find out how he wants me to handle it."

After I had used the bathroom, I returned to the same chair and once again my right hand and both legs were tied down.

The room I was in was approximately the same size as my office, which was 16' x 12'. There were two doors, one entered from the hallway, and the other led to a

243

connecting room. The flickering lights originated from fluorescent bulbs that hung from the ceiling. My guard for the night was the same guy Don had hit on the head and locked into a closet. He sat in a chair directly across from me, tapping his pistol on the palm of his hand, and staring at me as if he hoped I'd try to escape.

The pain in my head wasn't going away, but my senses were slowly returning. It wasn't going to be a comfortable night's sleep, so I began to mull over the situation.

Don and Shelley wouldn't be aware that I was missing until at least late the next morning. Even if they wondered where I was, they wouldn't know where to look. I had previously told them not to call me on my old phone number, and the new number had not been activated yet, so that was out.

Shelley would be the first to arrive, but she'd think I was with Amanda or Matthew, or out on an appointment. By the time Don came in around 11:00 a.m., they might begin to wonder, but they wouldn't know where to look. I left a note on my desk about the appointment, but only a name, not the location or a phone number. That information I took with me on a note pad. None of what I was processing assured me in the slightest.

For me to get out of there alive, I had to dream up an effective scenario, but I had no idea how I was going to do that. No matter how I looked at it, I didn't see a happy ending. I fell asleep with that unpleasant thought in my mind.

***

I had been awake for a couple of hours when the guy with the sunglasses walked in. My neck was sore from sitting in the chair all night, and I had lost feeling in both of my hands. I rubbed my left hand against my chest until I felt the blood start to return.

"We need some answers and we need them quickly." He stood over my chair. "Tell us where the information is and who else knows about it."

I stayed quiet, but paid a price. He struck me with a closed fist on my jaw. I brought my left hand up to protect myself, but it was too late, the blow struck me hard.

"I can do this all day if you'd like."

"No, I get your point." I rubbed my free hand on my jaw where I'd been hit. "I have a safe in my office. The disk is in there."

"Does anyone else have access to the safe?"

"No one else knows the combination."

"And that's the only copy?"

"If you remember correctly, you took the other one. After that, you killed Marsha Cummings, so there's no one else who knows about it."

He brought his right arm up to hit me again but must have thought better of it. He probably decided I wouldn't be any good to him if I were unconscious.

"What about your partner? He must be aware of what you have."

"He knows it's important, but he doesn't know what it relates to. I'm not even sure myself."

245

"This is what I want you to say to your partner." He handed me a piece of paper. "Read it to me so I'm sure you understand what it says."

I grabbed the letter with my left hand and read. "*I've reached an agreement with Ray Gilbert,*" it began. "*I've decided it would be in our best interest to hand over what I have, and in return, he's agreed to leave my wife, son and my business alone. I agreed to it, but I need your help.*"

He pulled out his phone from his pocket. "Now call your partner and read it like you just did. Tell him to bring the files here. If he tries anything sneaky, he'll never see you alive again."

He wrote down the address where he wanted Don to go and handed the paper to me. 3496 Wayzata Boulevard. I knew the location. We were in a warehouse a couple of miles from the Gilbert Headquarters building. I thought of a plan. "I'll only do it if I'm assured that Don will not be harmed and that Ray Gilbert will meet with me. I'm serious. He can leave as soon as I have my say. Those are my conditions."

"Your conditions? Who are you to be giving us conditions?"

"You're the ones holding all the cards. I just want to look Gilbert in the face one more time."

"I'll ask him, but first you need to arrange the transfer."

He handed me his phone.

"I can't use your phone," I said.

"Why not?"

"My partner doesn't like to be bothered, and has a

block on his cell phone that only accepts calls from people who are listed in his address book. Besides that, I don't have his number memorized."

He put his phone away. "Go ahead, call him on your phone, I don't care, but I'm going to listen in."

He pulled a chair next to mine and showed me how he wanted me to hold the phone so he could hear what we were saying. I pulled the phone from my pocket, turned on the power and called Don.

"Big Fella, I thought you weren't..." he answered, but I cut him off before he could finish.

"Don, listen to me. This is important." I read the note I was given.

"Okay. What do you want me to do?"

"I need you to go into my office and open the safe that's underneath the picture of a cabin on Lake Superior. The combination to the safe is CLM."

"CLM," he repeated.

"As in Cathy Linda Madden." I said the name slowly as if I was thinking of words that matched with the letters.

"I understand."

He didn't laugh or question what I was saying. That was a good sign.

"Take the disk and bring it here. Do you have a pen? Write this down." I read him the address I was given. "That's just east of Highway 169 on 394," I added.

"When do you want me there?"

I looked over at my captor and whispered, "What time?"

247

"He needs to get down here as soon as possible."

Don would need time if he understood my cryptic message. I was sure that he knew I didn't have a safe in my office and hopefully he'd understand the connection between what Cathy Madden said to him at her cabin and her initials being the same as the combination. Even if he did recognize the coded message that I was in trouble, he'd still have to drive to the 5th Precinct station and hope Pat Williams would be available when he arrived. That was a lot to wish for.

"How quickly can you get here?" I asked.

"You got me just as I was going into the shower. Let me think. I'll have to drive down to the office, take the disk from the safe, and then drive all the way out to Golden Valley. Somewhere along the line I'll need to stop and get something to eat, but I'll get over there as fast as I can."

I hung up and was about to slide my phone back in my pocket, when the guy with the sunglasses stopped me. "Give me that," he demanded. "I don't want you calling your partner and warning him when we're in the other room."

I made sure the power was still on and handed him my phone.

"If everything goes smoothly, maybe we'll all be home in time for dinner," he winked.

I didn't believe a word he said. Ray Gilbert had no intentions of letting me go. "I'll say this one more time. I get to speak with Ray Gilbert or the deal's off."

"Deal, what deal?" He looked at me as if I was

248

crazed. "There is no deal. You turn over the information that you stole from Ray Gilbert and we'll think about letting you live."

He pulled his Glock from its holster and pressed the barrel of the gun against my forehead. "It seems like an easy decision to me. Of course, if you don't give us what we want, you'll die, then your partner will die, and for icing on the cake, we'll kill your son and ex-wife. From what I hear she's a hottie, so we might need to have a little fun with her first."

My body tensed up, but I managed to portray a calm exterior. He went back into the connecting room, but I could still feel the cold steel of the Glock's barrel against my forehead. One flinch from him and my life would've been over. It wasn't a pleasant sensation and I had to make sure it didn't happen again.

THIRTY-THREE

MY CAPTIVITY HAD turned from bad to worse. It was a long shot that Don understood the true meaning of my call, and if he arrived and wasn't prepared, he'd be walking straight into a trap. To make matters worse, it didn't appear that Ray Gilbert would show up to meet with me.

I sat frantically using my left hand to untie my right, but the guy who tied the knot knew what he was doing. I gave up on the idea when I thought that even if I freed my hands and legs, I wasn't exactly a long distance runner and it wouldn't be long before one of the two men discovered I was gone.

The guy with the sunglasses entered the room. "Have you tried to call Gilbert?" I asked.

"And tell him what? He'd think that I couldn't do my job, and you were the one who was in charge. Tell me what's so important. If I agree, I'll relay the information."

"It's about the future of his political career. Tell him that I'm going to make him an offer he can't refuse."

"About Mr. Gilbert's political career? I think you're grasping at straws, but I like you," he said. "I'll talk to him and tell him what you said, just don't hold your breath waiting for him to show up."

He went back into his room and this time when he returned, I received some good news. "Mr. Gilbert surprised me, and was intrigued with your offer. He has a meeting he has to attend this afternoon; if it finishes before your friend arrives, he'll stop by. But he's not making any promises."

I was relieved, but the fact that Gilbert would only come before Don arrived, made me realize that he didn't want to be here when the transfer was made. It didn't take a genius to know what they had planned. They were going to kill us as soon as Don arrived.

After about one hour, he untied my hands and legs from the chair and allowed me to stand. He gave me a moment to stretch, before he tied my hands behind my back and pushed me against the wall. He waited next to me with his pistol in his hand. He must have felt there was a good chance that Gilbert would be coming, because he showed more interest in me than before the call.

***

I was getting tired of waiting. "What time is it?"

"11:45 a.m."

It had been almost two hours since I had spoken to Don, but it felt longer. The clock inside my brain was ticking much too fast. The longer I waited, the more anxious I became. I had to remind myself to breathe and

251

stay calm.

My mind wandered when I suddenly heard footsteps outside the door. It could be Gilbert, or it might be Don. My fears were answered when the door swung open. "Keep your gun pointed at his head," Gilbert said to his man with the gun. "If he tries anything, shoot him."

The other man who had guarded me overnight walked into the room when he heard Gilbert's voice.

If this were a movie, it would have been the perfect time for Don to arrive with the entire 5th Precinct and crash through the door. Unfortunately that didn't happen.

"You wanted to speak to me? Well, here I am." Gilbert stood in front of me at arms length and waited for my reply. "Tell me about this offer that I won't be able to refuse." His face was bloodless and his eyes were dark. It felt as if I was staring into a black hole.

I stepped closer, but both of his men quickly moved between us. "I want to tell you what a repulsive human being you are." That was all I could think to say. Not exactly original, but it was true.

He laughed. "Is that all? I was expecting more from you, that maybe you had changed your mind."

I stared in his face. "Changed my mind about what?"

"Nothing, it looks like I was mistaken." He picked up his briefcase and turned toward one of the guards. "You know what to do once you've secured the information from his partner."

He walked toward the exit and I needed to think of something to say so he wouldn't leave. "I know about

252

your plans to change our country and your desire to be the next president. It'll never happen. You're deluding yourself."

He stopped and replied over his shoulder without turning around. "Why do you even try to deny it? You know as well as I do that white people were created to lead and non-whites were born to follow. I thought that if anyone would understand what I'm trying to accomplish, it would be you. You've been a major disappointment to me."

That wasn't what I was expecting to hear and I was stunned. How could I be a disappointment to Ray Gilbert? "That's bullshit. Why did you hire me? I talked to Sergeant O'Hara at the 5th Precinct, and he told me he never spoke to you."

He finally turned around to face me. "You really don't know do you?"

"Know what?"

"Why do you think I came here to see you? I thought the offer that I couldn't refuse was going to be about your birthright."

My birthright? I was speechless.

"It's who you are. You're a natural born leader."

I was confused and Gilbert must have seen it in my eyes.

"The only reason I came here is because I felt I owed it to your father." He turned his head slightly like a teacher would speak to a wayward child.

"What does my father have to do with your misplaced delusions of grandeur?"

"Lieutenant John Crow was an inspiration to our organization. I'm surprised you didn't know that."

I tried to discern whether Gilbert was throwing me a curveball, or if what he claimed was accurate. Was he suggesting that my father was a white supremacist, a Nazi sympathizer and a believer in eugenics? I was shocked to hear it, but I had to admit that I didn't know my father well enough to say it wasn't true.

"That's bullshit."

"It's not." He took a step toward me. "John Crow believed that the white race was in danger of being driven from our homeland. All I'm trying to do is carry on his work by securing the existence of our people, and providing a beneficial future for our children."

"Is that how you justify it? What about Marsha Cummings' future? She was white, why didn't she fit into your plans?"

"This is going to be a long war that we're prepared to fight, and like all wars, there are causalities." He sounded as if he was giving a campaign speech. "Marsha was one of the first to die for the cause, but I don't expect her to be the last. That's not the way I would have preferred to end it with her, but she didn't leave me a choice. We gave her an option, but she refused to listen."

"You're pathetic."

Gilbert shook his head. "You should be thankful for what I did to help you with your career. You were a mess after getting shot, and it was my hope that you'd join us in our crusade once you knew the truth. Obviously that's not going to happen. You found Marsha Cummings and

254

I'm grateful for that, but now it's time for me to say goodbye."

He nodded at a guard and walked toward the door, but before he could get there, it came crashing in, and the police officers swarmed inside.

THIRTY-FOUR

"FREEZE!" I WAS never so happy to see anyone as when I saw Sergeant O'Hara and his men come through the door. His officers spread out around him with their guns drawn. "Drop it!" O'Hara yelled. "Drop your weapons and get on the floor."

One of Gilbert's men did as he was told and fell to the floor with his arms stretched to the side, but the guy with the sunglasses had disappeared.

Gilbert spoke with calm surety. "You're just in time officers. This man has threatened me and my men."

"Is that right?" O'Hara came closer to Gilbert. "Then why were your men holding the guns, and why are his hands tied behind his back?"

"Who's in charge here?" Gilbert demanded as if he had been wronged.

"At your service," O'Hara answered.

"I'll have your job, and after I'm finished with you, I'll sue the police force."

"Go ahead, this is still a free country, no thanks to you. But first I'm going to place a pair of handcuffs on your wrists and read you your rights."

O'Hara motioned two of his officers toward Ray Gilbert, while another one untied my hands. Gilbert didn't resist, but the level of his voice dropped. "I'd like to speak to my lawyer."

"All in due time Mr. Lieutenant Governor, all in due time, but first...you have the right to remain silent..."

I edged slowly into the other room to see where my captor had gone. The room was empty and the window was open. "Sergeant O'Hara, one of Gilbert's men has escaped."

"He won't get very far," I heard him say from the other room. He didn't seem to be in a hurry.

***

Don Hanson waited patiently behind a large oak tree. With the permission of Sergeant O'Hara, he had decided to cover the back of the building. He looked around and wondered what was going on inside, when he noticed a window being forced open.

From behind the tree, Don watched the guy with the sunglasses drop awkwardly to the ground. Before he was able to stand up, Don moved in and grabbed his arms from the back. Reaching under his arm, Don removed his pistol from the holster and slid it under his belt. "Going somewhere?" Don forced his elbows together until he groaned.

I walked around to the back of the building while O'Hara finished reading Ray Gilbert his rights. Sunglasses was lying on his stomach with both of his arms behind him. Don was standing with his feet on either side of his back, and holding on to his hands as if he were riding a surfboard.

The man screamed, "That fucking hurts, asshole!"

"I bet it doesn't hurt as much as this does." Don pushed harder and crossed the man's arms even farther. "No time like the present for a little payback."

As soon as he saw me, Don let go of his arms, grabbed the back of his shirt and pulled him up. Sergeant O'Hara appeared and the man called to him. "Help! This man is assaulting me."

O'Hara looked at him and then turned to me, gazing at my bruised face. "Is this the man who did the handy work on you?"

"I was just about to thank him when you arrived."

O'Hara looked at me and smiled.

"Well, don't mind me, I just came back here because I thought I smelled a donut truck around somewhere."

He turned his back and walked away.

Don grabbed Sunglasses. "Give him your best shot," he told me.

"Hey, man," he pleaded. "I was in the same boat as you. Gilbert is crazy! I had to do what he wanted or else he would have killed me. You can't hit a defenseless man."

Under normal conditions I would have agreed with him, but I couldn't overlook what he had done to Marsha Cummings and it sure didn't bother him to hit me when I was tied up.

"Like hell I can't!" I said.

My one punch landed solidly on his jaw and

knocked his sunglasses off his face.

While Don was still holding him, he tried to bend over and pick them up, but Don's foot beat him to it and crushed them into the ground.

Sergeant O'Hara came back to look at the man I hit. His jaw had begun to swell. "I guess that wasn't a donut truck, I must have been mistaken. He must have received that injury while he was trying to escape. I'll get one of my men to cuff him and take him to a patrol car."

Before that happened, I made sure I took my cell phone from his pocket.

THIRTY-FIVE

I WATCHED RAY Gilbert being taken away in handcuffs. By the time he was sitting in a patrol car, a small crowd had gathered and seemed to be interested in who he was. He smiled like it was all a big mistake and it would soon be cleared up, but for the first time, I saw a crack in his façade.

I turned to Don. "You had me worried, whether you understood my call or not."

"I didn't, at first, but then you told me to look in your safe and gave me the combination. Only you could think up something as convoluted as that."

"I take it that Pat Williams was cooperative when you contacted him?"

"He was like a kid in a candy store."

"Do you know if he was able to record the conversation from the software on his computer?"

"I'm not sure. Earlier, he turned it on while I was there, and we could hear you loud and clear. O'Hara has stayed in contact with him, and he's at his office waiting at his computer. Call him if you like, but if I were you, I'd have someone look at that cut on your head and the bruises over your eye and jaw."

I had forgotten about that with all the excitement going on.

"Maybe later."

Sergeant O'Hara yelled through the still-open window where Sunglasses had tried to escape.

"Crow! Get in here. I have some questions I need to ask – and bring that partner of yours with you."

I spoke to Don from the corner of my mouth. "I take it you had a chance to speak to my former Sergeant?"

"He's a real charmer. He reminded me of my old football coach. He talked, I listened."

I spent the next ninety minutes reviewing everything that had taken place, beginning with my first contact with Ray Gilbert. After I was finished, the Sergeant explained that he had just spoken to Pat Williams, and my conversation with Gilbert had been recorded.

"Now it's up to the District Attorney to decide how he'll proceed. To avoid the publicity and a long trial, he'll probably offer a deal to one of the men who grabbed you, and give them immunity if they agree to testify against Gilbert. If he can't get one of them to roll over, I doubt if he'll have enough to prosecute. Gilbert never really admitted to killing the woman when he was speaking to you, only that she was a casualty of war. There might also be a question if the recorded conversation can be used in a court of law."

"Are we finished?" I asked. "Are we free to go?"

"You can go, but are you going to be all right? It

looks like they gave you quite a beating."

"I'll be okay."

"I'm glad to hear that," he said sympathetically, but his rare show of emotion didn't last. His voice returned to the drill sergeant level I was used to hearing. "Make sure you and your partner stick around town for a couple of days. We might need another statement to tie up all the loose ends."

The same room where I had been held began to get crowded as word spread that the lieutenant governor had just been arrested. Reporters who must have been listening to a police scanner were filing in, and I had to look around to find Don. He was in a corner standing next to a young woman who was holding a microphone to his face. I walked over to hear what he was saying.

"When did you first believe that Ray Gilbert was a suspect in your case?"

"Darlene, is it?" Don was smooth. "I've been working on this for a long time. When I felt I had gathered enough evidence to go forward, I shared my findings with Mr. Crow and he agreed to look into it." He looked up and saw me behind the reporter and smiled.

"Here is someone you might want to meet." He waved for me to come closer. "Tony, this is Darlene, she works for the Minnesota Daily newspaper."

"Hello, Darlene," I greeted her then turned toward Don.

"We should get going."

"Okay," Don turned back to the reporter. "Why don't you give me your number Darlene, and maybe we can get together later for a private interview." He smiled and winked. "You know, just the two of us."

They exchanged phone numbers and Don followed me to the door.

THIRTY-SIX

RAY GILBERT WAS taken to the 5th Precinct station and charged with two counts of kidnapping. He was released less than two hours later when he posted a one hundred thousand dollar bond.

The next morning I drove to St Paul, to meet with Jordan Cook the State of Minnesota's lead attorney in their case against Gilbert. Cook started our meeting by explaining that Riley Thomas (Sunglasses) had offered to cooperate with the prosecution in exchange for what he hoped would be a reduced charge.

"We didn't promise him anything."

"Do you think he'll be helpful?" I wondered.

Jordan shrugged his shoulders. "He never met Ray Gilbert, nor spoke with him, until they met at the building where you were held. But, he told us he knew - through his contacts - that the lieutenant governor was the one responsible for hiring him. He might be a decent collaborating witness, but the evidence in this case is going to come down to the recorded message between you and Gilbert, and the fact that he came to see you when you were tied up. That's not a lot to go on, but Gilbert made a huge miscalculation by showing up to confront you."

"Will that be enough?"

"I've seen guilty verdicts with less evidence, but they didn't have the legal team that Gilbert will employ. One of the problems we have is that he only speaks in generalities on the recording and never admits to anything. You can make a strong case that he's a terrible human being, which I think you called him, but that's a long way from convicting him of a crime, especially murder."

"How about kidnapping?" I challenged.

Jordan shrugged again. "Your testimony will help, but we still need to see what else we can dig up. Thomas gave us the names and phone numbers of the people who hired him, but so far we haven't been able to locate any of them."

"So what happens now?" I asked, although I was pretty sure I knew where this was headed.

"Without a direct link, the murder charge is probably going to go away."

"So what are you trying to say?"

"Don't get your hopes up for a murder conviction. If we can pin a kidnapping charge against Gilbert, I'll consider it a victory."

I walked out of the attorney's office with an ache in the pit of my stomach. I was sure Gilbert was responsible for the murder of two people, but I had just been told that nothing legally could be done. The evidence was weak, and I knew it, but this case bothered me because it was personal.

One thing I could count on was that Gilbert's political career was over. All the negative publicity he had received when he was arrested would doom his plans to run again. Even if he was acquitted or came away with a lesser charge in the kidnapping indictment, his reputation was ruined.

***

As it turned out, Ray Gilbert never went to court. The state's lone witness, Riley Thomas committed suicide while he was in a cell. At least that's what was ruled. He apparently hung himself with a tied up sheet from his bed.

With not much else to go on, Gilbert's lawyers and the district attorney agreed to a plea bargain. In it, Gilbert would agree to immediately resign as the lieutenant governor for the State of Minnesota, pay a one million dollar fine and serve a year of probation, but he wouldn't have to go through a trial where his beliefs would be made public. When I heard about the agreement, I wanted to scream. A million dollar fine sounds like a lot of money, but to someone who is worth three billion dollars, it was a drop in the bucket.

***

I still looked forward to my bi-weekly visits with Matthew. It was amazing to see how fast he was growing up and how much he was learning.

Amanda and I decided to hold off on any further

discussions about getting back together. It was mostly her decision, but I understood and supported her reasoning. She wasn't prepared for what happened when Matthew was abducted and she wanted to distance herself from my work. We agreed that it would be best for Matthew.

EPILOGUE

AFTER THE PLEA bargain between Ray Gilbert and the State of Minnesota was released to the media, the phones at my office rang off the hook. Both local newspapers wrote favorable stories about my role in breaking the case and Sergeant O'Hara was keeping me busy with referrals.

Recently, after another long day at work, I fed Max, made myself a cup of tea and sat on my much-loved leather chair in the study. Clouds were rolling in; the local weatherman had predicted a storm would move in from the west. I was content to gaze through the patio door in the back of my townhouse and not have to think about work.

It had been almost a month since Ray Gilbert had told me about my father's views and I was still numb about it. I didn't know my dad well enough to say that it wasn't true, and in fact, what Gilbert told me might answer a lot of questions I had about some of his behavior. I wondered if my mother knew. She passed away nearly six years after my father was shot, and she never mentioned anything about it to me.

What I remember most about her was that she had a trusting heart. I appreciated how well she raised me, especially because she was forced to do it alone. But when it came to being street smart, she was naïve and probably wouldn't have understood her husband's beliefs, even if she had been aware of them.

Max jumped in my lap just as a flash of lightning lit up the skies and a crack of thunder followed. The promised heavy downpour began. I've always found rain to be refreshing and this storm did not disappoint.

As a young child I'd look forward to the first downpour of spring. Whenever a weatherman predicted a storm was moving into the area, I'd make a peanut butter sandwich on white bread and cut it into small pieces (so that it would last). I'd then bring it to the screened-in porch in the back of our house and I wouldn't take a bite until I saw the first drop of rain.

Winters in Minnesota could be cold, long and extreme. To me, springtime meant a new beginning for the wintered grass, daffodils and lilacs. Their fragrance would permeate the air with a sweet, floral smell. The spring rain was a sign of good things to come and a signal that new life was about to begin. It also meant that the accumulation of the snow's dirt and slime was finally being washed away. Maybe this rain would have a similar effect and wash away the dirt and slime of Ray Gilbert's beliefs, but it couldn't bring Marsha Cummings back to life.

She had desperately tried to get away from Gilbert,

but in spite of it she was murdered. I wished there was some way the legal system would have made him pay for her death, but at least he was forced to resign as the lieutenant governor and his political career was over.

I wondered how many more people were out there who shared similar beliefs.

I hoped there weren't many.

***

The more I thought about Gilbert, the more I didn't feel like staying home, so I gave Don a call.

"You want to go get a beer?" I asked as soon as he answered the phone. "I'm sure I can still drink you under the proverbial table, like I did the night of our high school graduation party."

"When I lived in Mozambique, a wise man once told me to make sure you have goals in your life, but don't make a mistake by setting them too high," Don replied.

"Let's find out if that wise man knew what he was talking about."

"I'll be in front of your house in a half hour," he said and hung up.